As always, th

Mom, who made me proud to be who I am today,
and The Sophie, the brightness in my life and the best self-rescuing princess ever. Of all time.

The Blame Game
by John G. Walker

Also available:

The Sincerest Form of Flattery
In The Details
Parts of the Whole

Acknowledgments

Hey, I remember you folks! You stopped by and checked out In The Details and The Sincerest Form of Flattery! And you brought friends! That's awesome!

So I imagine you're wondering what I'm going to say here that I haven't said already, and the answer is simple: I want to make sure those who have helped me get to where I am today get all the credit/blame they deserve. I'll probably miss a few people, and I know I'll catch hell for it, but you know what? I still freaking love you people.

First off, my mom. Yeah, she gets double thanks because, you know, she's my mom, and she's awesome. I wouldn't be the writer... hell, the man I am today without her help, her wisdom and her penchant for telling me not what I want to hear, but what I need to hear. Thank you.

Next, of course, is my niece The Sophie, who will always cause me to strive for greatness, so she'll always be proud to have an uncle who makes up weird tales and make sure she always knows that an imagination is a good thing, and she will know that she is my inspiration for being the best I can be.

The rest of my family, from my sister and brother-in-law (thanks for letting me vaguely use your likenesses!), to my grandmother, to my dad, all of whom have made me think, made me reach beyond who I am, to who I can be.

For my editor... Pryor, you're just awesome. Thanks for keeping the story straight in my head. This would have sucked without you. Words fail.

Starla Huchton, the graphic genius who makes the covers. Amazing and awe-inspiring. I always hope to write stories worthy of these covers.

To the rest of the Four Horsemen: Thanks for being my friends.

For my fans and friends on Facebook: I less than three you crazy folks.

To the RoosterTeeth community, especially the RTAD folks: I freaking love you awesome sexy party people.

As always, to my readers... Thank you for taking another chance with me into the world of the Chronicles. I have an idea of where we're going, really I do. It's going to be a little fun, at least for a little while longer. Thanks for sticking around and seeing where this twisted path leads.

By the way, usual disclaimer applies: Names and places changed to fit the story, blah blah blah. I did do some real research, though, and a good portion of the descriptions and events are from history and mythology. Yeah, I know; imagine me being accurate! Anyway, enjoy this latest Statford Chronicle, and I'll see you on the other side.

-John G. Walker
April 15, 2013

Chapter One

When you seek revenge, dig two graves. It's a cliché from one of the oldest civilizations on Earth. It may not have the brevity of the old standby curse "May you live in interesting times", but it does have a kernel of wisdom to it. I didn't subscribe to it personally, but considering the world around me, I knew in some places revenge was more popular than ice cream. Yeah, I didn't think being more popular than ice cream was possible either, but we mortals are a silly, vengeful lot at times, usually on days ending with the letter "y".

It had been a few months since my last big case, and things had gone pretty smoothly since then. By smoothly, of course, I mean I hadn't been beaten to a pulp by a pretender to the throne of Hell, or by a psychotic Russian who thought he was going to be a god before that. Any day I can wake up with little to no back pain is a good day, and one where I can shave without popping a couple painkillers beforehand is an awesome day. I had helped my friend on the Newport News police force, Jim MacPherson, on a quick job, then gone on a much-needed winter vacation to the gulf coast of Florida. Getting away was nice, and it was even nicer with company.

Still, as I was born mediocre-looking and not rich, I had to get back to work. Besides, the gods don't schedule their existences around me. I counted myself lucky I even got the week off from the weirdness.

That weirdness mostly included the Conclave, a

collective of deities who worked like the United Nations and were about as dysfunctional, and they were my main clients, and it was up to me to resolve any disputes they might have with each other or the mortal world. As an impartial mortal intermediary, I kept the omnipotent from smiting entire populations in fits of pique, and usually kept mortals from screwing up their lives when messing in the affairs of the gods. We really are crunchy and taste good with ketchup.

My title is the Keeper, which I think the gods chose because "whipping post" didn't sound as appealing. I had been in this illustrious position for a few years, and I found that things were getting a hell of a lot weirder as time went on. The gods usually didn't rub shoulders with us as often as they had been recently, but like all entities of any sentience, they just wanted to be known, to be acknowledged, to have someone say "Hey, you exist!" They had been getting a lot more chummy lately, and finding out why was on my list of things to do.

Granted, it wasn't terribly high on the list, but it was there. Somewhere. After getting a root canal with no happy gas and watching the director's cut of "Batman & Robin".

Okay, I really wasn't interested in finding out why things were getting weird, or why there had been sightings of a dark complected guy with four arms walking through the mountains of India, offering safe passage to all who traveled with him, or why some lady in Wales had started a cult of Epona to get infertile women pregnant, and it actually worked. I didn't really care. I had had enough on my plate the last couple of years without going on an international road trip to figure out what the gods were doing, and I didn't have to go. I already knew why: The gods really are crazy, and we mortals fascinate and entertain them; lucky us.

Regardless, it was out of my jurisdiction; the rest of the world would have to get along without the Keeper traipsing hither and yon. I had to earn my keep, though, and I had given my word I would keep things as mellow as possible between gods and mortals.

So it was back to the grind, and I was okay with that. I was actually relaxing that mild Tuesday, late on a February afternoon, getting in some reading and a couple of TV shows I usually missed. Hooray for the internet. Though I really kept the TV on for either background noise, news or video games, today it was for watching some recorded episodes of a local talk show. One of my guilty pleasures and scripted to a fare-thee-well, I still got a perverse sense of pleasure from the silliness. The other person in my office, however, did not.

"I do not understand how you can watch this tripe, Thomas," the spirit said, miming a lean against the wall. As he was incorporeal, he was actually against a picture on the wall and not disturbing it. "In my thousands of years, I have never seen such ridiculousness."

I laughed and replied, "Larry, you're not supposed to understand it." I rarely called him by his proper name Larrisimus, and it was usually not a good thing when that happened. "It's just something to entertain the masses."

"Thomas Statford, I do not know what you consider entertainment, but that," he pointed to the screen, which featured an all-out brawl with miraculously no one getting hurt, "is offal."

"Never said it wasn't," I said. "Just something to while away the hours until quitting time." I was actually anxious to get off work, since Suzy and I were supposed to go out, and things were getting a lot better between us.

"Ah yes," Larry smiled, his blond hair shaking as shook his head. "You and your ladyfriend are going to enjoy each other's company." He smirked. "You should have listened to me last year."

I rolled my brown eyes and tossed a convenient pencil at the spirit. It passed through his muted purple Jean-Paul Gautier suit with no effect, and Larry winked one of his blue eyes at me. "Blah blah blah, we had a falling out that was both our faults, we made up. Hey, I never claimed to be perfect. It happens." I chuckled and mused, "Don't know what she sees in me, though."

The spirit got a faraway look in his eyes as he answered, "Sometimes, Thomas, you do not have a choice in who you love, or who loves you. It just is."

His words touched something deep within me. Quietly, I said, "That was deep, Larry."

Larry's smile returned a bit. "It was meant to be."

I winced as someone onscreen threw a chair across the stage, which managed to miss everyone and not hurt a single thing. Throwing like that takes situational awareness, especially when you have a bunch of people in the way. I mean, sure, I could have done it, but I have had a bit of practice. "So what should I be doing, Larry? Pounding the pavement looking for a case? Boning up on some esoteric bit of knowledge that you think would be important in some obscure way? Can't I just have a slack day?" I went back to my book, the latest in that detective series Susana had told me about. It's apparently a universal rule that private detectives have to have some kind of sidekick, usually annoying but with some redeeming features. I had had plenty of time to read while recovering after my last case, a personal family matter I don't want to get into right now.

"Thomas, you have sat nearly immobile in that chair for over two hours, alternating between that book and that infernal machine with the foolish breathers," Larry declared, pulling himself away from the wall. "You have not been the same since your little vacation with Susana. Did something happen between the two of you? You are not in trouble with her, are you?"

"Not even a little bit." I smiled a bit.

"That is a unique situation."

I shrugged off the implication. It had been a good vacation, and I was certain Larry had enjoyed the freedom I had given him during my absence. As he was bound to me by forces beyond mortal comprehension, I had to give him special permission to go and do the things he wanted without a metaphysical leash. Everyone deserves a bit of freedom and Larry was no exception, as he wasn't some servant; he was probably the best, most loyal friend I could ever have. It was a vacation from the weirdness we all needed. The time I had been gone with Susana was good for the three of us, and I had told him to go and indulge himself until I got back. Though he didn't get a bit of the tan like I had gotten, I could tell the time away had done wonders for him.

After the credits rolled, I figured it was time to close up shop. No cases were going to head my way that day, and I just felt the sudden need to get out. Larry even looked impatient to leave, for all his words otherwise. I got up very suddenly, and sat right back down from dizziness. I made the attempt again, this time slower and steadying myself on my desk. That time I stayed upright. "I'm getting too old for this," I said to Larry, grabbing up my keys.

"You know little about getting old, Thomas," Larry replied, smiling slightly. There was something else in his eyes as well, and I couldn't quite put my finger on it.

"Coming from someone on the shady side of sixty centuries, I'll take your word for it." I started for the door, then patted myself down. Crap, forgot my phone. I went back to my desk to grab it.

I got halfway to the door when my office phone rang. Though I was half-tempted to let it ring since it was rarely good news, I decided to answer it anyway.

"Tom Statford Investigations," I said.

"Well, aren't we formal?" the voice of my lady, Susana Magdalena Iglesias y Marquez, lilted out of the receiver. "What's wrong?"

"Nothing, darlin," I answered, rather confused. I don't get caught flat-footed often. "What are you up to?"

"Just checking to see if we're still on for tonight. It's your turn for dinner and dishes." Susana was an amazing cook, but seemed to think I had some skill at it. I just thought it was because she wasn't the one cooking. Her Mexican roots showed through in her cooking, though, and many a night I had both loved and hated what she made. Loved because it was so good, hated because of what it did to me afterward. Damn, it was worth it, though.

"Last I checked, it was your turn," I retorted, a smile on my face, "and I had won a pass on it after those roses and the trip to that fondue place you love." I heard Larry clear his throat and ignored it.

Her laughter, musical and full of life, answered me. "Pendejo, you should know better than that." Even though I knew what the word meant, it always gave me a chill hearing her speak Spanish. Seriously, I was like Gomez Addams without the suit and mustache. "Besides, you know I make the rules, and the rules say you owe me dinner and dishes tonight."

I shook my head, stifling laughter. "And just what rules are those, darlin?"

"The rules that say if you don't, that office bed you got is going to be used for awhile."

My mouth couldn't hold back the laughing anymore. "The lady knows how to bargain."

This time she chuckled. "Who said we were bargaining?" I hate it when she gets me like that.

Larry caught my eye with a wave. "Thomas,

we need to go right now," he said severely. When I gave him a look, he hooked a thumb at the door. Warning bells started sounding. Larry wanted to leave with a quickness, and even though I was talking to the love of my life, now that I wasn't focusing completely on Susana, my feet were itching to get out the door. Not to see Susana, but to just get the hell out of the office, out of town, out of the country. Something had Larry wanting to leave too, as I saw him try to start to fade away, but get drawn back by his binding to me. He couldn't leave unless I gave him the go-ahead, and something in my head wanted me to tell him to run his translucent ass off. That's when something else clicked.

"Babe, why did you call my office phone?"

The surprise made it through the phone lines. "I thought I called your cell. No wonder you answered the phone like that. I'm sorry." I heard her shrug it off. "You still aren't getting out of cooking."

"I won't be doing anything if I don't get out of here," I said, and that felt a bit too true for comfort.

That's when the worst cliché of any private detective's life happened. You've seen it in a thousand movies: a slow saxophone playing in the background, a foggy night, moon shining down, and the tough-as-nails, hard-boiled private investigator sits there with his bottle of scotch and the broken memories that litter his past. He's contemplating another night with his best friends Jack and Jim on the rocks, then passing out in a haze of booze. Every moment he's just sitting there, thinking about some past failure, or whatever got him through the

scene. The music hits a crescendo.
    And then she walks in.

Chapter Two

The handset lowered from my ear, and I could hear a faint tinny voice coming from it, and I knew that voice from somewhere, but for some strange reason, I couldn't place it. I lifted the mouthpiece of the phone back to my mouth and muttered something that may have used the words "call", "back" and "later" before dropping the phone in the cradle. There might even have been a goodbye that was less "good" and more "bye". I had no idea; all I knew was that someone had just walked in, and she had trouble written all over her.

Eyes trained by my mother and numerous shootouts went over every square inch of her as she stood at the doorway. She was tall for a Chinese woman, probably an inch or two below my five-ten without the heels. With them, she was a bit taller than me. Ephemeral was the best way to describe her, with smooth skin nearly glistening like ivory under the light, arms exposed to the elements by the sleeveless black dress she wore, a thing that would run anyone a few thousand dollars just to reserve. There was a fur stole around her neck, and it didn't look fake. She had long black hair, slightly curled at the ends, over her left shoulder, so black and thick all you wanted to do was plunge your fingers into it, just for the sensation and sheer pleasure of doing it. Diamond chips on her ears, fine gold link chain at her neck, huge rock on her left hand's ring finger, with the left hand clutching a small purse, diamond tennis bracelet on her right ankle, black leather high-heeled shoes on her feet. My eyes went back to her face, seeing the blood-red lipstick, the make-up accenting her cheekbones, and the bemused smile. Absolutely beautiful, gorgeous, intoxicating.

So, in a nutshell, dazzling trouble in a black dress rather than a devil in a blue dress? I was glad for the former; I'd had enough of the devil to last me an eternity.

With that, I pushed away the aesthetics and picked her apart mentally. It helped to calm my hormones, and the fact that she was probably the second-worst thing to walk into my office cooled me down even more. I'd already had my ass severely kicked in the prior two months; I wasn't due for another beating until at least Christmas. Once I had her marked as trouble in my head, I looked at her completely objectively. The more I looked, the more I saw, and the less I liked. Something told me even letting her in was a bad idea, but it was too late. I had had my chance to leave before. Once I had her in my mind, which took all of about twenty seconds, I broke the silence. "May I help you?"

"I hope so," she said, and her voice was like pure silk each word dripped from her crimson lips like water off a ducks back revealing a deal more about her. Amazing what three words can reveal. "I'm looking for Thomas Statford. He's a private investigator. This is his office, yes?"

"I hope so," she said, and her voice revealed a ton more about her. Amazing what three words can reveal. "I'm looking for Thomas Statford. He's a private investigator. This is his office, yes?"

Bringing myself back to reality, I nodded.

"Yeah, this is his office. Why are you looking for him?" There were a couple more things I was noticing about my visitor, neither of them good, and they got my danger sense going into overtime.

She sighed, pert breasts rising and falling with the exhale. "I was told he could help me. Do you know where he is?"

I shrugged my shoulders and said, "Yeah. He's me. What can I do for you, ma'am?" I made my way behind the desk and sat, kicking my feet up.

"You?" Her tone was both mocking and incredulous. Not the first time that tone has been applied to me, and likely not the last. "You're Thomas Statford? There must be some mistake."

"Were you expecting Sam Spade?" I retorted. "Trenchcoat, fedora, half-smoked cigarette next to a half-drunk bottle of whiskey?" My laugh escaped me. "Sorry I don't fit your idea of a private detective, but you could do worse."

The look on her face was pure derision. "Oh, please. You can't be who I'm looking for; you're a fraud."

A fraud? That got my eyebrows raised. "On the contrary, lady, I'm a great many things. A fraud is not one of them." I pointed to the chair. "Now, if you'll sit down and tell me what you need, we can get this started and done quick as you want."

My words seemed to derail her somehow; something was definitely wrong here. She was debating whether it was worth it to stick around. Coming to a decision, she sat in front of my desk, crossing very long, very smooth legs in my direction, and they were legs that could, in the words of the Rolling Stones, make a grown man cry.

Hey, I'm a guy, and I'm observant.

She reached into her purse and pulled out a piece of paper with two fingers. I heard a muted clink from the purse but thought little of it as she leaned over and placed the paper in front of me. It unfolded itself on my desk, and I saw that it was a cashier's check. Scratch that: it was a very generous cashier's check for fifty thousand dollars. I looked from the check to her face, a half-smiled formed on her lips, as I said, "My birthday was a couple of months ago, ma'am, not that I don't appreciate the offer."

The lady quirked an eyebrow. "The money is for two things: listening, and telling me who I am. If you can do both, it's yours."

I hate being quizzed, and I hate when some chick shows up and acts like she knows more about me than I know about her. It was time to show her something I learned from one of my childhood heroes: a guy named Sherlock. "Who you are? I've never seen you before in my life." As she reached for the check, I said, "I do know you're from the Chinese mainland, probably the Qinghai province by your accent, even though you left China at an early age." She pulled her hand back. "You're in your late thirties, and take great pains to look younger. I don't know who does your makeup, but they know how to put you together." That the fingers of her left hand went to her ears and jaw confirmed it. "Your English sounds like you went to Oxford rather than an American university." I put my hands behind my head, as I let the details filter through my mind and drew conclusions. I went on.

"You've been around the block once or twice, and got the treasure to show for it, and been to the altar at least once." The ring was probably worth more than the average sports car, and looked just out of the box. The tan line was nearly non-existent under the ring, offsetting the crimson of her nail polish. "Fairly recently, I might add. Your current husband is either dead or dying, probably from old age, which is okay by you, since you're getting all his money, and there aren't any kids, probably because he was too old to have any ram in his rod." I smirked. "Or you were too smart to get caught like that." She inhaled sharply, and seemed about to stand up in anger. I smiled mildly and commanded, "Sit down, trophy. You wanted me to tell you who you are. Be careful what you ask for."

Standing anyway, she hissed, "Are you through insulting me?" Her words were sharp, and if they had been capable of cutting me, I would have bled to death.

"The truth isn't an insult, lady," I retorted, "Now's the part of the deal where I listen to you tell me how I was wrong and why you're in my office, testing me like I'm supposed to be working for you already." I put my feet on the floor and leaned forward on my desk, my fingers intertwined. "So you can either start talking, or you can take your check and wibble-wobble your narrow ass out of my office." I smiled again. "You've got three minutes."

It took her fifteen of the one-hundred-eighty

seconds to bring herself back from most likely leaping over the desk and hooking my eyes out with her well-manicured nails. I've seen the look before; it wasn't the first time. When she could speak again, she could have frozen lava with her tone. "I needed to make sure you were worth the visit, Mr. Statford. I have very little time."

That silky voice turned to ... "I needed to make sure you were worth the visit, Mr. Statford. I have very little time."

"No kidding. You've got a little over two minutes."

"You've the manners of a goat. Were I not pressed for help, and a few other factors, I would not be in this backwater town, dealing with the likes of you." Before I could retort, she reached into her purse, again with two fingers. I watched her toss something metallic into the air toward my desk, and my reflexes nearly made me grab at it. It would have been grabbed, had I not gotten a very bad feeling from the piece of metal flipping through the air and Larry screaming in my ear not to touch it. Still, it was a close thing, and my hand was half-reaching for the object anyway as it landed flatly on my desk, not spinning, just a muted thump.

"My name is Jiao Shen-jing, Mr. Statford, and I need your help to find out who murdered me." Her voice was completely devoid of emotion, almost monotone.

That caught me a bit flat-footed. Her lack of any reaction surprised me, especially given certain obvious problems with her statement. "Okay, Miss Shen-jing, you just got yourself an extension," I said, gesturing back at the chair, "as long as you can explain to me how you can say you're dead when you're in front of me, talking and breathing. I don't deal with ghosts very often; my proton pack is in the shop."

Jiao sat back down, the words seeming to have drained the fight out of her. "I did not say I was dead, Mr. Statford. I said I was murdered."

"So there's a difference, huh?" I shrugged. In most situations, semantics and word games bored me. "Well, then, let's start with the obvious: Do you have any reasons that someone would want to murder you? Your charming personality, perhaps?"

I could see she was maintaining her cool exterior at great cost, so I mentally vowed not to push her anymore, at least not too badly. A guy has to have a little fun. "I will ask you to be somewhat less abrasive, Mr. Statford; even with my abbreviated time left, I am not without those who would make sure you leave this life before I do, at least early enough to hold the door open for me." As I said, a charming personality. I leaned back in my chair and gestured for her to continue, making a note of her choice of words. "Thank you." Jiao took a deep breath, her assets very nearly on display for a moment. It was a rather tight dress, and I was rather relieved when she exhaled.

"Mr. Statford," she continued, "I received that coin four days ago. Do you know what it is?"

It was my turn to sigh as I was getting tired of the constant tests, but I took a look at it anyway, just to see if I could find out more about this mystery woman. The coin itself was dull metal, but didn't seem to be heavy enough to have caused such a thump when it landed. I almost expected a dent in the dense wood of my desk, but from what I could see, there was nothing. Like most antique coins, it had a square cut out of the middle, for whatever reason. There were ideograms, Chinese of course, and I couldn't read them. The ideograms and the metal itself looked worn, anyway, as if the coin had been handled by thousands of hands. I couldn't see any dents, nor any filing marks that might have indicated the ideograms had been restored or replaced. "If I had to guess, I'd say it was an I Ching coin. Old one."

"Very old, Thomas," Larry piped in. "This might be two thousand years old if it is a day."

"You speak correctly, spirit," Jiao said, stunning the hell out of me.

I looked closely at her. "You can see him?" I said as Larry said, "You can see me?" It would have been funny if it hadn't lent credence to her declaration of death.

"I am one of the dead already, Mr. Statford," she said, her voice oozing smugness it didn't need. "I've been seeing many spirits already the last four days." Jiao shuddered, her first non-haughty emotional response since she had walked in. "More than just spirits, in some cases."

To Larry, I said, "Why can she see you?"

The ghost shrugged. "I do not know, though it is possible she possesses a gift to see into the ether. Some of you breathers have a talent for that." He seemed reluctant to continue until I gave him a look. "It is also possible that she is correct, and she is one of the dead." Larry's mouth quirked in a smile. "Stranger things have happened."

"Contrary to what my friend here says, ma'am," I said, "you seem to be very much alive." I started to move my hand to the Colt Python revolver I kept as a backup gun in my desk. "So it might be a good idea to start telling me why you think someone's murdered you, and what an ancient I Ching coin has to do with it."

Jiao took another deep breath, but fetching as the first show was, I wasn't fetched this time. It was hard to tell what was an act, what was real, and what were just her going through the motions of an act. I actually felt sorry for her in that moment; she didn't even know who she was anymore, just a figure of what some man years ago told her she must be so she would be comfortable. "As you said, I am from China, and I was born to very modest means. My early life was hard, so I made my way out any way I could. My choices may not have been the best ones, but they got me away from that farm."

"How long ago?"

"Long enough that I barely remember what that little girl was like." The words were stone, and didn't allow for much interpretation. "I married well twice, and have managed to secure a future for myself. I did what anyone in my situation would do. I won't be blamed for what I've done."

I let that statement go for the moment. "So where does the coin come in?"

"In the last few weeks, several of my---" she hesitated, then continued, "business partners have come up dead." She flicked a glance at the coin, the dull metal reflecting no light. "They were in possession of a coin similar to that one. Within eight days of receiving it, they died."

"How many so far?"

"Four, two within the last week." She could have been telling me she was having pie for dessert instead of cake or she liked carnations better than roses for all the emotion she showed. I had an inkling of how she got out of China, and it wasn't as a foreign exchange student. "The coins themselves all look the same, though the inscription is too hard to read, and the ideograms are very old."

"This one reads 'No blame for the blameless,'" Larry put in. He had been examining the coin intently, but never getting close enough to touch it. "You do not have the others?"

"Officially, the authorities have them," Jiao said. "Unofficially, they have disappeared within hours of their recipient's death. I don't know where they are. They are dangerous."

"How so?" I said. "I mean, I know what they do. They tell the future and assign blame, right?" I got a nod from Larry and a rather brusque nod from Jiao. "How are they dangerous?"

"Four people die, each having received one of these coins eight days before their deaths?" Jiao looked at me incredulously. "Don't tell me you think it's just coincidence."

"No, but I don't much believe in cursed artifacts," I retorted. "The powers that be don't like things like those screwing up the mortal world. They have enough power as it is, and the gods are already seen as trouble at best, useless at worst."

"She is correct, Thomas," Larry said. "This is an object of some power, though of a curious kind." He moved closer to Jiao, who seemed to almost expect the spirit to dote on her every word. "You said you received this coin? How?"

"It was left in a box on my desk," she answered coolly. "I made the mistake of opening the box and dumping the contents into my hand. Had I known what was in it, I certainly would not have done it."

"You knew what this coin meant when you got it?" I was starting to find some holes in her story, and they weren't small ones.

She shook her head, her hair nearly a solid mass as she kept her eyes on me. Very disconcerting, to say the least. The lady was being very careful to keep our eyes locked, and that didn't help me feel much better. Usually when someone was trying to keep my attention somewhere, they were really wanting it diverted from elsewhere. "I had seen it from the reports, but never before then."

My eyes searched hers, trying to find something besides disdain for people who weren't her. Something was just off about her; I couldn't quite put my finger on it. I couldn't tell if she was being false about the story itself, but the answers to her questions were completely canned. She had worked on these responses for awhile, and they were almost second-nature to her. Either she had looked for help from someone else already or she had rehearsed this scene until she had it by rote. I don't like someone lying to me, and I certainly don't like someone who thinks they can throw a lot of money and cleavage around and expect me to dance.

"So why come to me?" I finally asked. "I'm hardly the only private investigator in the book, and you ain't from around here." I drawled the last bit. "Why me?"

Jiao shut down hard. "I don't think that's any of your business, as long as you get paid properly. You will do as I say, as long as I'm paying you."

First a fraud, now a mercenary. I was starting to feel like she didn't respect me. "Okay. We're done here." I picked up the check and put it in my pocket. "Go be murdered somewhere else, lady." With that, I turned my chair on its swivel base towards the television and turned the thing on, catching the last few minutes of a soap opera. I kicked my feet up on the desk, purposefully keeping from looking at her, even as she started talking to me.

"How dare you!" she screeched. "That's my money!"

"Which I earned by listening and telling you about yourself." I kept my voice as hard as I could. "That's what you said, and I did it. My job is done, and as far as I'm concerned, and since you think I'm little more than a mercenary fraud, listening to the bullshit you were slinging, I more than earned it."

I could almost see her mouth open, the red lipstick accentuating her lips as she gaped at my impertinence. I felt good about it, actually. "You insolent little peasant! I told you the truth!"

"Lady, you told me half of what I needed to know. If you won't tell me everything, then we have no business to discuss." My hand snaked into one of my desk drawers as I turned back to face her. The walnut grips felt good and solid. "I don't appreciate lies, blatant or by omission. So either start talking or get the hell out of my office."

She seemed to emotionally shut down, almost like a light switch except more abrupt. "I could have you flayed alive." The flatness of her voice was scarier than the promised threat. "It would be a trivial matter for me. I know people who would be delighted to end your pathetic little life."

"Yeah, and you'd end up just as dead from whatever brought you in here in the first place." I smiled back at her, not wanting to let her know how badly I was rattled by her words. "No one wins, everyone loses, and not a single damn will be given either way." My smile became wolf-like. "What's worse, lady, is I disappear and it looks funny, whoever does the disappearing will have a lot of very high-powered hounds after them, and they will not stop until they are a greasy spot in the footnotes of history." I kicked back, making a dismissive gesture. "Look, we can threaten each other all day and all we're doing is burning daylight. Talk or leave. Your choice."

Jiao sat back, glaring at me with barely-contained contempt. I looked back mildly. She was afraid of dying, but I thought she was even more afraid of showing weakness. It didn't matter much to me; I was ready for her either way. Finally, she seemed to come to a decision.

She chose wisely.

"I was visited by someone two nights ago," Jiao began. Her voice was halting, somewhat fearful now. "Someone I had stopped believing in a very long time ago. He told me about you. Mentioned you by name."

I smiled slightly. The time had passed for the clenched fist. The velvet glove had to come out. "I'm flattered. A client?"

"I don't see how that would be possible." Jiao's voice dropped to a whisper. "It was in a dream."

Oh lovely. "You'd be surprised who my clients are. Who was it and what did he say?"

Jiao slouched slightly, becoming less the statuesque Chinese beauty and more the scared little girl from the backwater farms of China. This wasn't an act; I was staking my life that it wasn't. "It was Ehr-Lang, and he said that he could not help me, that I had passed from his protection, and that you could help."

"Ehr-Lang is the god who chases away evil spirits," Larry provided. "The great restorer, he is called. Very charming fellow."

"So this Ehr-Lang," I said, "whom I've never met, says you're no longer under his protection? Were you ever?"

Jiao seemed to show some emotion, a mixture of relief and disbelief. "You mock me?"

I shook my head. "Hardly, lady. Like I said, you'd be surprised who my clients are. Were you ever under his protection?"

"When I was a girl in my village, before I... left, I would pray to him for rescue in secret." That pause was speaking volumes. "When I did leave..." She trailed off.

"You stopped praying to him," I completed. "It

wasn't quite the rescue you thought it'd be, I take it."

"No." And there was a hell of a lot of pain in that one word. That bit of sympathy I had for her that had left before started to sneak in again. "Ehr-Lang said that I was to find you, that you were a guardian for mortals."

"He mentioned me by name? Again, I'm flattered." I turned to my ghostly friend. "That's what they're calling me now?"

Larry quirked a small smile. "One of the kinder labels, yes. You have built a bit of a reputation in the Conclave, Thomas. There has not been a Keeper of your particular stripe in recent memory."

"'My particular stripe'?"

"You have no qualms about breaking the rules to uphold what is right."

I nodded sagely. "Yeah, that's me, fighting the forces of evil, et cetera, et cetera." To my client, I said, "So what else did Ehr-Lang say?"

"I had six days to find you, or I would meet Chu-Jung. That was two days ago."

"The god of fire and executions," Larry provided. "Not someone with whom to trifle."

"Sounds like a wonderful guy," I muttered. I sat back, the gun staying in its drawer. "So let me see if I have all this straight. You got an ancient I Ching coin, which other people you know also got. They died, and you were visited by a Chinese god who told you to find me, and that you had six days to find me, or you would meet a Chinese fire god who does executions on the side." I looked at Jiao, my hands folded on my desk. "That about sum it up so far?"

Jiao seemed near tears, and in fact a couple had already fallen, tracking black mascara down her cheeks. I had to admit, that was a nice touch. "I know it sounds unbelievable, but it's the truth!" She put her face in her hands and sobbed quietly. "Why don't you believe me?"

"I didn't say I didn't believe you, ma'am," I said, pulling out a box of tissue. "I just wanted to make sure I had everything correct so far." I got up and walked around the desk to her. She looked at me with something like hope and pulled out one of the tissues. "This is probably one of the best referrals I've ever gotten, so no worries." This was also probably one of the best acting jobs I'd ever seen, which was a worry. I twisted my body to put the box on my desk, then turned back to her. "I'll take the case, but I'll have to check out a few things first. Leave me a number for where you're staying, and I'll contact you."

"Of course, Mr. Statford." She put a number and address on a business card from her purse. "This is my mobile number, and the room I'm staying at the Omni." Lady knows how to stay in style.

"I'll likely have a few questions for you when I contact you, so don't be surprised." I backed up a step so she could stand. "It'll be okay," I offered. I didn't know whether it would be or not, but hey, someone had to be the bright ray of sunshine for the lady who thinks she's been murdered by a Chinese fire god.

"What will you do with the coin?" she asked. "I

cannot leave it with you, but you might need it."

"One second." I took a few pictures of both sides with my phone, with Jiao kindly flipping it so I could see both sides. "The wonders of modern technology," I smiled. She took the coin and put it back in her purse. I unconsciously let out a sigh of relief when it was out of sight. I didn't even like having the pictures on my phone. "I'll be calling you tonight."

"Thank you, Mr. Statford," Jiao said, with what seemed to be a genuine smile. She stood and put her arms around me in a hug. "You have done me a great service."

Involuntarily, I hugged back. "Don't break out the champagne, lady. I haven't done anything yet." The scent of her perfume filled my head; it definitely wasn't rose water.

"Tonight, then," she said.

And then things went from out of the frying pan and into the gaping jaws of Death herself armed with a bazooka.

"Tonight, huh?" A new voice ripped through my office, a female voice. "I'm certain he'll have plenty of time for you."

I pushed away from Jiao and saw Susana standing there, hands on her hips and murder in her eyes. Have to love great timing.

Chapter Three

And then from the gaping jaws of Death herself armed with a bazooka, things get worse.

Susana had glared at Jiao as she left the office, then as soon as the door closed I got the evil eye from the woman I love. My girl had apparently raced over to find out what was wrong, especially since I hadn't answered my cell phone, which was on vibrate and I didn't hear it, and my office phone hadn't been hung up all the way, leaving the line open.

Of course, I didn't find out any of this until after the love of my life came in like a spirit of vengeance, full of fire and destruction and pretty much a desire to kick my ass sideways. Larry had bailed in a hurry; he had seen Susana on a roll before.

"You hung up on me because of another woman? What the hell is wrong with you?" Susana then went into a fully automatic barrage of Spanish that I didn't have a prayer of translating. The most I caught was a word or two here and there, mainly "*puto*" and "*pendejo*" with a sprinkling of "*marecon*", which really added flavor. Needless to say, it wasn't very complimentary to me. I let this continue for about five minutes, just so she could get it out of her system.

"She's a client, babe!" I shouted, not meaning to shout, but it was the only way I figured she would hear me over her bilingual blasting. "That's all, nothing else."

"Oh, you are so full of shit!" Not the worst

thing she could have said to me, but it ranked up there. "That *puta* had her hands all over you, and you sure weren't fighting her! Where were you going to do her? On your desk?"

I sat back against my desk, pinching the bridge of my nose with my fingers. Biting back the retort I wanted to send her way, I took a deep breath and let my own anger bleed out. "She's nothing more than a client. That's all. It was a hug. That's all."

"Don't lie to me!" Susana was taking this really badly. "I know who she is!"

"So do I. She's some rich chick trophy wife who is under a death threat. What's so godsdamned bad about that?"

Susana was about to launch another attack when my words penetrated. She looked at me with slowly dawning comprehension. "That's what you think she is? Some 'trophy wife'?"

I exhaled heavily. "Yeah, that's what I got from her. Don't know what else she is, but she's rich enough to drop fifty grand on my desk just to get my attention."

"So you don't know she's a hooker?"

There are a few sentences that can get someone's complete and undivided attention. "I'm on fire!" is one of them. "You just won a bazillion dollars!" is another one. "She's a hooker", though, definitely ranks up there as far as getting my attention. "A hooker?" I repeated dumbly.

"A madam, to be exact." Susana sat in the same chair Jiao had sat, but I didn't think it a good idea to let her know. "We nearly busted her three years ago for running a brothel out of Phoebus."

I should have known, and some of Jiao's mannerisms were making more sense with this piece of information. Funny how that works. "I think I saw that in the paper."

Susana made a disgusted noise. "Yeah, for one day, then it was never heard about again. Right after the bust, we got the word that all our evidence was from an improperly executed warrant, so she got to walk." She leaned forward on her knees and looked up at me. "Tommy, she's a very bad woman. I mean, really bad. We call her the Dragon Empress for a reason. The things we found there, the way the girls were treated, it was horrible." I didn't say anything. I couldn't say anything. "You've seen those shows where they show behind the scenes of a bust, right?" I nodded. "Those are the ones we'd rather see, where we aren't finding girls living in their own filth, cleaning up only long enough for some piece of shit to hump them for five minutes. The ones who are strung out on opium or heroin or whatever else they can addict the girls to are the lucky ones." Susana's eyes went far away as she remembered. "When we tried to get the girls out of that place, they didn't want to go. They just wanted their next fix. Those girls didn't care what happened to them as long as they could shoot up. They'd have killed their own mothers for one more hit. Those little girls fought us when we pulled them out of the walls they were hidden in, because they knew they were going to lose the only thing that would help them forget what had been done to them."

"She was involved?" I asked gently. I had never heard her so upset.

"Involved? Shit, Tommy, it was a nice little family business. Her building, her car in the back lot, and we had enough circumstantial evidence that any judge with cojones would have convicted her." Susana sat back in the chair, her hands over her eyes. "Eight of the girls died that day at the hospital. Complications from extended drug and physical abuse. Eight out of a dozen, and the bitch got to walk." She snorted. "Probably wrote the whole thing off as a business deduction."

Susana looked again at me, and I knew what she was going to ask before she said it. "If she's going to die, maybe it's a good idea to just let nature take its course."

I would be lying if that thought hadn't occurred to me during our conversation. "I can't, Susy. It would be wrong."

"More wrong than her helping a bunch of little girls, none of them over fifteen, get addicted to drugs and pimped out? You have a screwed-up sense of wrong, Tommy."

"It's more than that," I said, and I hated that I was having to defend someone like this. Jiao and I would have a long talk about this. "She came to me because I was recommended by someone on my side of the weirdness."

"So? Can't you let one case go? She doesn't deserve it."

"I can't say I'm inclined to disagree with you, babe, but I don't get to make that determination. I have to find out why someone's made her a target, and I got the recommendation from on high."

"Just following orders, huh?" Susana's eyes

narrowed, and I knew I was in for it. "Well, I imagine you have a lot of work to do for your new client, so don't let me get in the way."

"Susy," I began, "it's just a case. I don't---"

"No, Mr. Statford, it's not just a case." Oh shit. "It's about you choosing to help a sub-human piece of filth because of your 'job' rather than just letting the puta die."

"Now hold on a godsdamned minute!" I roared.

"You enjoy your night, Mr. Statford." Susana stood up and walked to the door. "I hope you're happy with your choice."

And with that, she walked out, managing not to slam the door so hard that the wood split, but it was a close thing.

Funny how life can turn on its ear in less than an hour.

"She left less than pleased, I take it," Larry said when he returned. His arrival was about three minutes after Susana departed.

I hadn't moved from where I had been sitting since Susana left. I was stunned at how things had just completely fallen apart in so little time. "You could say that." I made my way around to my chair, pulling my laptop close to me. Going through the archives of the local papers was pretty illuminating in regards to my client, in that there was nothing about a brothel in nearby Phoebus, but plenty about her being a pillar of the Asian-American community. According to what I read, she had donated thousands in money and goods to the under-privileged in the Hampton Roads area. What jumped out, though, was the teen outreach program she ran for runaways, and I had to wonder about her recruiting methods.

Not for the first time, I wondered just why I was doing what I was doing. Susana was right. This woman was an evil woman, and I was likely being suckered into helping her. While I didn't advertise my usual clientele on my business cards, certain people in the know were aware of my in-between status with gods and mortals. Someone with enough money could easily cook up some story and next thing you know I'm eyebrow-deep in trouble again, and one of the few people who could help me had just walked out of here probably ready to spit on my grave. Needless to say, this was probably not one of my smartest moves. Then again, I'm not known for consistently making smart moves.

"Did you get anything from her that this was a lie?" I asked Larry. "If I'm going to be in hack with my girlfriend, it had better be worth it."

Larry shook his head. "For what it is worth, Thomas, it was genuine, or as genuine as she can be. She does have a taint around her; that much is not in doubt."

"So what is in doubt?" I sensed that unspoken question.

"Whether it was actually Ehr-Lang who appeared to her, and whether that coin actually appeared out of thin air on her desk."

I pushed back from my laptop; it was hard to reconcile the lady in the awards with the demon Susana had described. I didn't doubt my girl's word, but it would be hard to convince other people the humanitarian they celebrated was a madam. As it was, I had too many unanswered questions, not enough data, and I knew that the plural of anecdote wasn't data. What made things worse was, if I believed Jiao, she had maybe four days to live. Oh well, I just love working under pressure.

What I don't love, though, is being taken for a ride.

I had my coat on as I left the office, making sure I locked up. A chill had fallen in the early evening, and I figured it was going to get even colder before the night was over. The sun was already on its way down, bringing a darkness to the world that didn't help things. I would likely pay for my siding with helping Jiao, and Susana never made things easy.

Regardless, I had made my decision, and this seemed like an easy case anyway. I just needed to find out who sent someone involved with human trafficking a cursed coin. I mean, you couldn't just find coins like that on eBay.

My first priority, though, was to get some more information from my erstwhile client. I had watched the same shows Susana had mentioned, and if Jiao was involved in prostitution and worse, I would be dealing with some very rough mortal customers, and I don't get any special protections like I do from the gods. I would need to be cautious, which wasn't my strong suit.

Yeah, I know that comes as such a surprise.

I pulled out of the parking lot and made my way to the on-ramp for the interstate. It was just before rush hour in the middle of the week, so I managed not to get snarled up too badly as I merged onto the highway. Probably would have saved time if I had gone the roundabout way, but I still needed a bit to chew things over in my head.

Jiao. I knew she was trouble from the minute I saw her, but for whatever reason, I decided to help her. This lady was probably one of the worst things to ever happen to me, yet there I was, off to try and slay dragons to save her. Not the best option, but when you're in my job, you do what you have to do.

Besides, it had been too long since someone had tried to kill me; I was starting to feel unloved.

I made it to her hotel, the Omni in Newport News. It was sixteen floors plus the penthouse suites of pure luxury, and I guess I shouldn't have expected otherwise. The lady screamed ostentatious, and the No-tell Motel wouldn't fit her M.O., any more than wearing Jean-Paul Gautier or actually having a plan that didn't possibly call for my malicious wounding would fit me. I pulled into the parking lot, trying to keep from hitting cars that were worth more than the cashier's check I had in my pocket. There were knots of people outside, most of them the younger set, and I made sure to park the Black Beauty far enough out in the lot to keep from getting dinged up any more than she already had. I had kept the 1998 Chevy Tracker going over the years, and treated her as well as I could. Parking was difficult on that score, as there were cars everywhere that seemed to have the same idea.

After a few minutes, I managed to get a good

spot and park. The wind had picked up, bitterly cold over the blacktop, made worse by what looked like a light misting of rain starting. I certainly knew how to pick the timing for visiting a client, as it had gotten dark quickly and the clouds obscured the anemic light of the quarter moon. Even the lights in the parking lot seemed muted as I made my way to the lobby past a bunch of loud kids who seemed to be celebrating one thing or another. School of any kind had long since passed me by, so I didn't know if it was some kind of dance or whatever kids did these days. They seemed to be throwing small noisemakers at each other, which didn't do much for my nerves. Too easy to mask the sound of a distant gunshot.

I shrugged off the sense of foreboding as I made it to the lobby. It was like something out of the movies, with sweeping staircases, crystal chandeliers hanging from the ceiling, and soft carpeting everywhere. The Omni had done some extensive remodeling the last few years, and it looked like the decorators had taken some inspiration from Hollywood, as I felt like I was walking into the Dolphin Hotel from the movie 1408. That movie was based on a Stephen King story, which did absolutely nothing for my sense of well-being considering I was probably dealing with something much worse than a haunted hotel room. I didn't even have Samuel L. Jackson as backup; that would have made me feel a lot better.

The whole place was the lap of luxury, with marble staircases, planters of exotic flowers, bellhops wearing their uniforms, the offspring of the incredibly wealthy parading around in ridiculous attire that could have fed a small city for a year. I didn't want to stay here any longer than I needed. With a low-voiced request, I had Larry watch the outside, in case someone decided to crash the meeting. Whether it was cops trying to bust her again or her possible business partners wanting to remove her from power, I didn't want to get caught flat-footed, as I'm not as spry as I used to be.

The room number on the card was one of the penthouse suites, of course, so I didn't see a need to bother the hotel staff. The elevator opened up easily, and as I pushed the button to begin my ascent, I just had that hinky feeling, that sense that no matter what I did, this would not end well for anyone. Things would probably go downhill a hell of a lot faster than they were, and it seemed there was already an ACME booster rocket strapped to my ass as I did the slalom in Aspen. I had my pistol with me, which gave me a bit of comfort, but when you were heading into an unknown situation with someone who alternated between begging you for help and threatening to flay your flesh from your body, having a division of tanks backing you up would have helped more.

After the way things turned out, two divisions of tanks along with a bazooka for me would have been better.

I'm not sure what I was expecting as the elevator opened, but it wasn't burning footprints in the floor. That definitely made things more interesting, as in "Oh crap, this is bad" interesting.

Without a thought, I pulled my Beretta, thumbing off the safety. I'm not sure what good the gun would do, but it definitely made me feel a bit better. There was a scent on the air, the smell of burning pork, and I had smelled it before, not very long ago. As I squatted down to check the footprints, I heard a thump from the room at the end of the hall. It had to have been loud, as the door was closed, and I knew these doors weren't some cheap plywood. I barely had the chance to begin standing when I saw the door buckle outwards, towards me. As I threw myself flat, the oak door shattered with a huge explosion, with the limp form of a suited man flying over me to crash into the metal doors of the elevator. He slid to the floor in a soundless, boneless heap, his facial features mangled, blood drizzling from what was left of his eyes and nose and ears to the carpet. I stayed on the floor for a moment, the explosion of sound playing havoc with my hearing and balance. It took me a couple of minutes to regain my senses, and a shake of my head to clear the cobwebs. I didn't even bother checking for a pulse as I half-stood and crab-walked into the penthouse, knowing I was too late to do anything but too damned stubborn not to try.

I've said it before and I'll say it again: I hate it when I'm right.

The room that had once been beautiful, was in shambles. As I walked in, I had to step over another suited man, his form shattered from having rebounded off the door before his partner destroyed it on his way out into the hall. I was careful not to step in any of the puddles of blood that had formed on the floor. I made a slow circuit of the entire penthouse, looking for signs of life elsewhere and finding none. There were small fires everywhere, the flames in cuts that covered the walls and the furniture. I could see several heavy chairs had been crushed, parts of them smoldering, while a couch and loveseat had been cut in half cleanly, almost like a laser, the halves pushed casually to the side by someone a lot stronger than I was or ever would be. The burning footprints went from one side of the main room of the penthouse to the other, the spacing even, not seeming hurried.

Whoever it was, whatever it was, it was stalking its prey.

From where I guessed the bedrooms would be, I heard a quiet mewling, then silence. The doors were closed for the moment, and I dreaded what I would find. Something in my head told me that whatever was in there was not going to make for a better day. That something also said that if I opened those doors, I would likely be in something over my head, and I was making my own decisions about being involved in something that absolutely didn't need to concern me. That voice also said that there was likely a dead or dying woman behind these doors, and she wasn't long for the world, and until I opened that bedroom, her death would be all on her. If I turned that knob, then like the song says, it would be nobody's fault but mine.

So of course I kicked open the doors, my gun at the ready. I couldn't have done otherwise.

She was dead, all right.

Jiao's lifeless form was on the floor motionless. She was in some kind of ivory silk robe with a similar color nightgown underneath. The robe was open and trimmed with gold, and the nightgown wasn't moving at all. The nightgown itself had ridden up a bit, showing her legs. The flaccid muscles would soon stiffen into rigor, which was something I didn't want to be around to see. Her hair was splayed around her head in an ebony halo, framing the rictus of pain on her face with all too clear perfection. I could see a small mist of red on the bodice of the nightgown, probably from where she coughed her last breath, and a deep dark crimson welt on the pale skin of her chest, just about where the heart would be. The flesh wasn't smooth there, either; there was a depression in her chest, about fist-sized. Her lips were red, and not the artificial red brought by lipstick. There was a thin line of blood dripping down the right corner of her mouth. Those were the only bits of red on her. I didn't need to be a doctor to figure out the cause of death; it had already been explained to me a couple of hours prior.

Around her were larger spots of red, probably where she spat blood from her mouth once or twice before she rolled over and breathed her last. The burnt footprints stopped at her feet, which were bare and pedicured. I made a circuit around her, careful not to touch anything more than I had already. I was noticing more and more with the body than on first glance. The palms of the hands were burnt, blisters formed on the palms, as was the sole of her right foot. In the burn marks were ragged ideograms, which probably had meaning to someone who could read Chinese in a mirror. Other than those marks and the depression in her chest, I couldn't find anything else done to her.

I squatted down, almost wanting to brush the nightgown down to preserve her modesty. No one deserved to die in such a manner, even if she was half the monster Susana made her out to be. I also wanted to close her eyes, but even that would have contaminated the crime scene worse than I probably already had. Granted, I was pretty much in the clear for this murder, but I didn't need any more drama than I had already brought on myself.

As I put away my gun, I took a closer look at the body. In Jiao's right hand was the coin, and the left had a couple of deep scratches on the web between the thumb and forefinger. I had had those scratches myself many years, though no longer thanks to practice on the range. Anyone who didn't know what they were doing with a gun would have those marks. Swiveling to my right, I could see the gun, slide locked open on an empty magazine, that had probably been in her hands at the last moments of her life laying there beneath the bed. I checked the walls of the bedroom and could barely see the holes Jiao's bullets had put there in a panic. Even to the last, she had fought her fate, for all the good it did her.

Knowing I was probably going to pay for it later, I popped the coin out of her hand with a pen from my pocket. I then picked it up with a small handkerchief, making sure I never actually touched the metal. The coin was cold, even through the cloth of the handkerchief. Jiao couldn't have been dead more than a few minutes at most, plus the heat that caused the blisters should have done something to warm the metal, but no. It was cold.

Cold as the flesh that held it.

I put the coin in the left back pocket of my jeans and stood slowly. There was nothing else to be gained here. I had failed a client, and I didn't even know what I had done wrong in the first place. You know, other than accept her case even when she apparently was on a deity's hit list. Of course, as far as I was concerned, the case was over. My client was dead, and I had less of an idea of what was going on than I had when she first walked in. There had to be something I was missing.

I did a look around the room, trying to figure out the dead woman behind me. The only things really out of order were the body, the footprints and the bullet holes in the wall.

Check that. The window had a very nice round hole melted into it, about four feet in diameter. The edges of the glass were still glowing slightly, which meant I had missed Chu-Jung by only a couple of minutes. I can't say I was unhappy to have not run into him, but it still meant I had a very dead client.

That brought another click: Jiao had said she had four more days. Either she lied to me, which wouldn't have surprised me very much, or her patron god had lied to her, which would have surprised the hell out of me. The gods, regardless of their pantheon, followed rules. Those rules might not make much sense to us mortal types, but the rules were there, and they stuck to them no matter what.

Everything else seemed to be in its place; the bed was still made, and the covers weren't even turned down. I could see out the window to the back parking lot, where quite a few party-goers were still gathering. When I got to the make-up table, I saw the usual implements women use to make themselves beautiful. Mascara, eyeliner, blush, lipstick; none of which was helping me. There was a folder full of paper on the table, and I flipped it open with my pen, scanning for any kind of information. I needed something to start making sense.

These were the files about the four other dead people who had apparently run afoul of the I Ching coins, if Jiao was to be believed. I didn't try to pronounce the first names, but the family names and the causes of death were exactly the same: massive coronary thrombosis, or, in English, their hearts exploded. Two were very old men, from Beijing, and looked like they had crawled every step of the way. Duplicate deep-set eyes in leathery faces, frown-lines very apparent, one with a scar on his forehead. Twin brothers, according to the pictures and the records, and they had done some very shady things over the years, if the folder was to be believed. The headings on most of the papers said INTERPOL, which did nothing for my peace of mind. With other information reading from the FBI, I got the inkling that these two were likely under high scrutiny, and more to the point, their deaths were likely celebrated by law-enforcement officials everywhere.

The other two files were thinner by half, which I thought was explained by the youth of the second two. From what I was reading, though, the only reason the folders weren't thicker was the combining of charges onto fewer lines of paper. One male, one female, both with similar names, but with the same ages. Twins. Again. Similar everything, it turned out, especially when it came to crime. Not even out of their forties, and according to what I was reading, they were suspected of enough murders, kidnappings, maimings, assaults, and various other felonies that the sun would be a cold, dark cinder in the sky before their sentences were complete.

None of this helped me, though. All this meant was I had five bodies, linked by blood and choice of vocation and the fact they were dead. I was just as stuck as I was before. The case had barely begun and already being stuck was starting to become a bit of a recurring theme for me, and I was hoping for a break.

Then I looked at the mirror.

Tucked into the frame of the mirror were several photographs, probably the only bit of real humanity this woman allowed herself. Several of the pictures had what looked like family members, which wasn't that odd, but Jiao seemed to be alone in most of the pictures, and she was smiling. Smiling at Nauticus in Norfolk. A sunny smile at the Museum of History in Newport News. Smiling at the Hampton Bay Days. Grinning at Busch Gardens. She was solo in all those pictures, too. That she was alone was weird enough, but smiling?

Something was different about the smile, too. This Jiao was warm, and real, and the smile didn't strike me as something manufactured for the camera. Using my pen, I lifted one end of a picture of just Jiao to look on the back.

"Son of a bitch," I breathed.

Written on the back of the picture was a name: Deng. The date on the back a few months prior. Above the name was a designation.

Sister.

Words trickled back to me, specifically what Susana had said about it being a family business. Maybe I hadn't lost all my leads after all. I pulled the picture of the sister and put it in my coat pocket, well away from the coin. No need to tempt fate more than I already had, as I had probably missed Chu-Jung by maybe two minutes. It was time to go.

That sentiment was confirmed when Larry appeared at my side, his eyebrows raised in alarm as he said, "The authorities are here, Thomas." He took a look behind me at the body, his face screwing into a moue of disgust. "Oh dear."

"Yeah, that's one way of putting it," I replied. I moved quickly out of the bedroom, trying to erase the picture of Jiao dead, her heart exploded in her chest, laying on the floor, a victim of some kind of theistic assassination. My mind conjured her alive again, then showed how she had probably been killed.

Chu-Jung shows up, big as life and twice as badass. She sends her goons to defend her as she heads to the bedroom for her gun. The god probably got shot at a few times, or even shot, but with no effect. Bullets don't react well to deities. He grabs one by the skull and squeezes, not letting the flames do anything quite yet. No, he's saving those for his real target.

I pushed my way into the stairwell, bracing myself for a blaring alarm. When none sounded, I shook my head. No wonder the cops were coming. The fire department would likely be right behind them. I started taking the stairs down two or three at a time while my brain continued the show, whether I wanted it or not.

Goon number two watches his buddy's head get crushed, the scream muffled by a mitt the size of a Thanksgiving turkey. Figuring wrongly he's next, he jumps on Chu-Jung, maybe trying to take him down, choke him out, it doesn't matter. The god finishes crushing the first guy's skull, taking his time, then drops him to the floor. To Chu-Jung, it's barely registered that something has hold of him and is trying to stop him from his goal.

The more of the show my brain put on, the faster I went down the stairs. I had ten flights to go, and I knew I'd have to be careful when I got to the ground floor. I couldn't count on logic prevailing when the cops found the body and Our Hero in the same building.

I already knew what happened to goon number two; from the speed with which he went through the door, his insides were probably crushed into jelly. The only thing keeping him together was the suit. While I was down on the floor deafened, Chu-Jung got into the bedroom, got shot at, and got his target. Most likely he reached into her chest through the flesh and crushed her heart while she kicked and grabbed at him. Simple and direct, and probably fairly quick. The burning of her hands and foot were likely forgotten in the pain of her heart's destruction. Then, at the end of it, the executioner placed the coin in her hand, not as a message since no one would understand it, but likely as a way of completing the ritual that had brought about the deaths of five people so far. After that bit of theater, Chu-Jung goes out through the window, leaving a mess for the mortal authorities to find and not giving a sweet shit about it.

When I reached the ground floor, I took a couple of minutes to catch my breath and clear my mind. The last thing I needed was to be out of breath in a hotel crawling with cops and three corpses in a penthouse. That would be what the detective's manual would call "suspicious". I asked Larry to take a look through the walls and let me know what was going on. I counted three before he came back.

"The coast is clear for the moment, Thomas," he said, "though I would recommend you hurry. There are quite a few uniformed police here, and they do not appear to be in a talking mood."

I slowly pulled the door open a crack, again expecting an alarm and getting nothing. I wasn't about to question my good fortune; hell, I had pushed my luck enough over the past few minutes that I briefly thought about getting a lottery ticket. Why not?

Larry hadn't been kidding; there were a hell of a lot of cops running around the enormous front lobby. I was probably about twenty feet from a gaggle of them as they looked to be comparing notes about something. That made me somewhat confused, especially since I had made it all the way down to the ground floor without seeing a single uniform. Usually the stairwells were covered when cops decided to swarm a place.

Not wanting to tempt fate anymore, I waited for my chance to make a hasty retreat. The ground floor was pretty bare right then, and there were clear lines of sight from the cops to my door. That didn't bode well for me getting away unseen. I was up a certain creek without a paddle if things didn't start to go my way with a quickness.

The elevator doors across from the main entrance opened, all three sets, and a torrent of noisy partiers streamed out. They flowed over the lobby and the cops in a rush, and the loudmouths were drunk as lords almost to a man. The loud noises got the attention of the uniforms, which gave me enough time to slip out of the stairwell and into one of the groups singing some nonsense song that I couldn't place off-hand.

I had about fifty yards to cover to get outside, and I couldn't count on this group to go the entire distance. Upon closer examination of my living camouflage, I found they were dressed in brightly colored, almost flamboyant silks embroidered with gold thread. Something was ringing at the back of my mind, but it was drowned out by the kids starting to sing a very rough a capella version of "Don't Stop Believin'". They were a mixed bag of ethnic backgrounds, but they had a few things in common: the average age was barely-legal, the blood-alcohol content was yes, and they couldn't sing worth a damn.

As they stumbled and bumbled one way, I finally broke off in another direction, moving from group to boisterous group. I even joined in the revelry, at least verbally. Being the quiet one in a bunch of drunks usually gets people looking at you, and I've found that in a group of loud assholes, everyone notices the silent asshole. Twirling a girl around in my arms helped move me closer to the exit, and got a laugh out of her and her friends. I needed to stay invisible for another few seconds as I made my way through the doors. I don't think I actually drew a full breath until I was actually outside, and not a moment too soon.

That was when I heard a bunch of alarms and loud cracks from inside. Either the noisemakers were military-grade, or some idiot was shooting off a gun inside. I didn't care; I was clear and free to get the hell out of there. I even had the temerity to smile a bit as I made the parking lot at a fast walk. If I could get back to the office, I could find Jiao's sister and maybe save her, then find out who was pulling the strings of a god to do some wetwork.

And maybe I could bring peace on earth and goodwill towards man by buying the world a Coke.

As I threaded my way through the suddenly running people, I turned a few things over in my head. While I didn't think anyone on the Conclave's side had anything to do with the why of Jiao's and her family's murders, they had a hell of a lot to do with the how. It rather boggled my mind. Usually mortals served the gods, not the other way around. This stank of mortal involvement, too. In the world, nothing is more vindictive or hungry for vengeance than humans; it's in our nature. This kind of killing was personal, too. There were a dozen different ways to have killed these people and made sure they were dead, all through mundane means. I mean, a bullet through the brainpan or a dagger between the ribs kills some poor bastard just as dead as a deity crushing the heart. To quote Richard Dreyfuss, this means something.

Of course, it wasn't a pile of mashed potatoes; it was some mortal bending a god to their will to do their dirty work. That meant one of two things: power, or leverage, which were pretty much the same thing.

I briskly jogged to the Beauty, hoping that whatever cops I knew on a first-name basis hadn't seen her on the way in to handle whatever the hell had broken up the party. Larry was doing a quick spiritual once-over to confirm what I already knew. A god had just directly killed a mortal, and for some crazy reason, it was being overlooked by the Conclave. Something like that made my spine crawl. That's probably why I didn't notice the red car next to my black one, or the red car's door opening as I put my key into the Beauty's door.

"Get in the car, Tom." Susana's tone brooked no argument, nor did the fact that she had her gun out make me feel any better. As if it couldn't get any worse.

Chapter Four

This night was not turning out to be one of my finest. There I was, leaving the scene of a celestial assassination, with evidence of the crime no less, there are cops and drunks everywhere, a bunch of gunshots were going off in a luxury hotel making said drunks scatter like roaches and put the cops on edge, and my pissed-off possibly ex-girlfriend was standing there, her gun out, looking ever more angry than I had seen her in awhile, and telling me to get in her car.

So what do you do when you're in such a situation?

If you're smart, you get in the car. Unfortunately, one thing I'm not is smart all the time.

"Suzy, I don't have time for this," I said. Arguing with a woman with a gun definitely doesn't make me a MENSA member, but I honestly didn't have time for it. "Let me go."

"Tommy," she whispered, "if you ever trusted me, trust me now and get in the goddamned car." She pulled the hammer on her pistol halfway back as she pulled the back door of her Toyota open. The meaning was rather clear.

I ducked my head and slid into the backseat, muttering, "Oh yeah, we need to talk." She barely gave me time to get my legs in before she slammed the door, effectively locking me in. Susana's Toyota was one of those modified types where the doors in the back had no handles, and there's bulletproof glass between the back and the front seats. The glass was a new addition, which made me wonder what else she had planned. I folded in on myself, pulling my coat around me and lowering my head. To say I was pissed was an understatement. Yeah, I may have gone against her ideas of right and wrong, but this was beyond mortal ken, a phrase I hated because it was true.

Someone came up to her as she stood outside the car, her gun back beneath her coat, apparently. The parking lot was dark, so I couldn't see who was talking to her, and at that point, I didn't give a damn. Susana and I had been through a hell of a lot, and I was giving her a hell of a lot of leeway right then. I mean, sure, I had blamed her for cheating on me with another woman, shot her in the stomach to stop a psychopath from becoming a god, caused severe damage to her car in an attempt to prevent Armageddon, and now made it look like I was siding with a (now-dead) scumbag human trafficker/madam over her, but it's not like I had done anything really bad to her.

Yeah, I know. I don't buy it either.

I saw the visitor duck down to take a look in, but Susana stopped him, so I didn't get a look, not that I was really interested at that point. This was starting to become a pain, and I was most likely under a time constraint. There was another young woman with a target on her back, and while I may not be able to stop a freaking fire god, I might be able to figure out just who was calling the shots. Sure, the girl might end up dead, but I could probably stop further murders.

Maybe.

Possibly.

Okay, not likely, but I could at least find out what the hell was going on.

After another five minutes of cooling my heels in the back of Susana's car, her visitor left, heading toward the hotel. I was a slow-burning fuse then, trying to keep myself from exploding when she got in the car. My eyes winced shut from the sudden light, which didn't improve my mood. Patience isn't always my virtue, but right then, I knew I needed to keep a clamp on my emotions. There were two reasons for this: One, she may have been wrong, but I loved her and she deserved the benefit of an explanation, or at least as much of one as I could give her; and two, she had me in the backseat of her cop car while she was wearing a gun and I couldn't get out of the car without her help. Just a case of being boned heart and body.

The driver's door closed, mercifully extinguishing the light. I blinked rapidly to bring my vision back somewhat. When I could see again, there was Susana, turned around and looking at me over the front seat.

"That was Parkinson," she said, referring to the guy who had just left.

"Chief Parkinson? What's he doing here? Slumming?" I was not number one on the chief's hit parade, especially after the high-profile suicide in the county lockup the year before. That I had been present at said suicide made things exponentially worse. It also hadn't helped that I had stirred the pot a bit, but what's a nemesis for?

Susana sighed. "There was a tip that some idiot

kids were going to cause some trouble over the Chinese New Year celebration. Seems to have been a bit accurate from what we can tell."

"But what's he doing here?"

"Outreach fundraiser for the Asian-American community." Susana sighed again. "Tommy, we need to talk." I opened my mouth to point out that I had said the same thing only a few minutes prior, but she held up a commanding finger. "Not a word til I'm done." My mouth slammed shut so fast I thought I was going to amputate my tongue. "Thank you." Susana took a deep breath and began.

"You were right." I opened my mouth again but closed it after a warning look from her. "I admit, I don't know what you did before we met, and probably not even half the stuff you did after we got together, and probably never will." She was right, and I never would tell her. "I'm a cop. All I want is the bad guys to stop doing bad things. Dead pretty much means they stop doing those bad things, and if there's anyone in the world who deserves to be underground, it's the Dragon Empress.

"It isn't right, though. I became a cop to dispense justice, not revenge." Susana looked out over the parking lot, then back at me. "You were looking at the big picture. I wasn't. Anything that can scare the Dragon Empress is something everyone else should be afraid of."

Susana smiled. "What I'm trying to say is I'm sorry, and you were right."

Oh boy, did I feel like an asshole. "It's okay, Susana. I do understand how you feel. Believe me, I understand."

"So you saw her?" Susana's voice was guarded, but she smiled a little. I was forgiven provisionally.

"You could say that." Something in my voice must have bled through.

"Was she busy with a client?" You could have frozen steam with her tone.

"Not exactly. She had an unexpected guest." I sighed and looked away from Susana. "She won't be dodging any more court cases."

Susana bit her lip. "Wow. So she's dead?"

I nodded. "Along with two of her goons. I figured the gunshots were what brought the boys in blue."

"They're here because of the tip and Parkinson begging for money." She massaged her temples with her fingers, her eyes closed tightly. "Oh shit, Tommy. You sure have great timing."

A chuckle escaped me before I could stop it. "I wasn't planning this."

"I know, but you still have great timing." Susana looked back at me. "So how'd she die?"

"From what I could tell, the same thing whoever else was involved in her little racket did: massive coronary." I didn't want to tell her about the god likely reaching into Jiao's chest. "It wasn't painless."

Susana nodded, more in recognition of the statement than satisfaction. "So your job is over."

I shrugged. "Maybe. There are a couple of things I want to check on, but as far as Jiao Shen-Jing is concerned, there's nothing else for me to do."

"Okay. I'm sorry about earlier, by the way. Parkinson was coming and I panicked. I called you a confidential informant. He hates getting involved with actual police work." She got out and let me out of the backseat.

"Thanks. I didn't have the stomach to deal with him tonight."

"He really hates you." Susana hugged me, and I held her close. "Watch your ass."

"Hey, as long as I have you, my ass is already watched." I laughed a bit as I kissed her. "I should be done with looking into this stuff by the weekend."

Susana let me go to the Beauty. "Did you find out anything? About who's behind it? Any leads?"

I paused a moment before answering. "No, nothing really. Just a dead woman and two dead men. No leads to speak of." I smiled, pulled out my keys and got in. Not exactly a lie, but she wasn't equipped for taking on a god or someone who could command a god. Of course, neither was I, but I at least had some protection. Susana, not so much.

"Good. See you tomorrow? Parkinson is going to have us working overtime on this tonight." She smiled at me, and I returned it. "You still owe me."

I laughed, knowing how lucky I was to have her. "Yes, dear. I'll be back at the office tonight." I turned the engine over. "Te amo, bella."

Susana actually blushed and flapped her hand at me. "Get outta here, gringo, before I handcuff you." She raised an eyebrow. "And I promise you won't like it as much as last time."

"Tease." I put the Beauty in first and drove off. I didn't often get the last word, but it was nice to do it every now and again. I checked the time and tried to remember the date. It wasn't too late, and I just needed some information.

I took out my phone and dialed up my other cop friend, Jim MacPherson, or Mac, to his friends. Mac was a homicide detective for the Newport News police department, and was one of the best, most honored and most honest cops to ever wear the badge. He had a perfect case-clearing rate, and he helped me out with getting me consulting gigs for the police.

I made sure I called his cell rather than his office line. If Parkinson was still mad about last year, Mac was probably feeling the aftermath. Sometimes it sucks being my friend, I know.

Mac picked up after two rings; I could hear someone singing in the background. "Hey, Tommy. What's up?"

"Not much," I lied.

"Uh-huh. How much trouble are you in this time?"

"Surprisingly very little for the moment. How's Dinah?"

"She's fine. Doing the dishes while singing along with the radio. I was helping before I got a call from a private detective friend who hasn't been over in two weeks who's probably going to ask me to compromise my integrity."

I sighed as I turned right onto George Washington Memorial Highway towards Jefferson Avenue. "Has it been that long?"

"It has. What do you need, Tommy?"

"Just information about a Deng Shen-jing. Female, Chinese national, thirty-five." I rattled off a few other details, including spelling the name. "Just need to know where to find her. She's likely in a hell of a lot of danger."

"Shen-jing? I know that name."

"Her sister is known to my girlfriend."

It took him a beat to get the reference. "Oh hell, you mean the Dragon Empress?" Mac whistled. "You want me to get SWAT ready to bail you out again?"

My mocking laughter was hollow. "You're a riot, and I wouldn't have needed SWAT if someone hadn't sneezed and scared the chimera." That was a rather ridiculous story for another time.

"Uh-huh. So how soon do you need it?"

"Soon as you can. I'm grabbing a quick bite before heading back to the office."

I heard Mac fumbling with something, then coming back to me on the phone. "Give me about fifteen minutes or so. See you this weekend?"

"Most likely," I said as I turned toward the mall. "I'm hoping to have this wrapped up by tomorrow."

He laughed loudly. "Yeah, sure. I'll be in touch." We said our goodbyes and I made a run for the border. Sure, it wasn't the healthiest thing in the world, but I didn't want to chance waiting for a table at a restaurant, and I had miles to go before I slept.

I was finishing off my second taco when my phone went off about a message in a bottle. "Talk to me, Mac," I said, swallowing quickly.

"Sorry I took so long," he said. "I almost couldn't find her."

That was weird, and I said as much. "Did you

have to go through INTERPOL?"

"Nope. They never heard of her. What's more, NCIC hasn't, either. She's never had so much as a parking ticket. What's more, she's a naturalized citizen."

"Okay, so she's a naturalized citizen. How long has she been in country?" I took a bite of my burrito.

"Ten years. Nothing out of the ordinary about her application as far as can be told, other than it got approved quicker than normal. She was here on a student visa, went to ODU, graduated with honors, got a job at the Smithsonian." I could hear papers flipping on the other end of the phone. I muted my end of the conversation to finish my meal and take a quick swallow of soda. People who eat on the phone when they don't have to just irk me. "Um, she's pretty much been a model citizen."

I unmuted the phone. "As compared to her sister."

"Dude, leave the Dragon Empress alone. She's not just evil. She's evil and crazy. The guys down in Special Crimes have boxes on this woman." There was some shuffling, and I knew Mac was moving to a more private area. "She's a very hands-on type of killer, and she's not very squeamish from what CSI reported."

"Bad?"

"One guy was found spread over a thirty mile radius in about as many parts, and they still haven't found all of him. That was four years ago."

"Well, that's not something anyone's going to have to worry about from now on." I figured I might as well tell him; Mac would probably be called in on the case anyway. "She's dead. All the way dead."

Mac exhaled loudly. "So that's why my captain wants me to come in tonight. Anything I should know?"

"Call it natural causes. Calling it an act of god would be too much." I asked my last question. "Where is she?"

"Not a clue. I didn't have enough time to find out." Mac covered the mouthpiece, then came back, saying, "Hey, I gotta go. Dinah says hi."

"Tell her I said 'What up, yo?' Be safe tonight, Mac, and make sure you call it natural causes. No need for the tongs to get their hair up." I referred to the gangs of Chinese descent who had started to be a bit more prevalent in the last couple of years.

"No problem. I have better things to do than get killed. You be careful, too. I have a badge and a whole department to watch over me. Who watches over you?"

I ignored the question. "Later, Mac." I hung up and pondered my soda. The demon had a human side, it seemed. Not a total surprise, but Jiao hadn't struck me much as a humanitarian. The thing was, if Jiao had gotten her coin earlier than she'd said, did that mean her sister had also gotten a coin, and was she already getting a visit from the god of fire?

Maybe I didn't need to worry about her. Maybe I just needed to find out who had gotten these coins, track them down, and go from there. Why screw around with symptoms and instead just go for the cure? That would make more sense, of course, so I did the only thing I could think to do.

I would take the coin where Indiana Jones would say it belonged: a museum.

Chapter Five

The only local museum I knew that could handle something of the apparent antiquity of the coin was in Norfolk, which meant I had to haul ass across the water. Located on the waterfront, the Virginia Museum of Ancient History had been around just short of forever, it seemed. I had probably spent a year total over my lifetime, first as a nerdy student who thought the exhibits were cool, then as an adult learning about the beings I called clients. Knowledge is power, and when you're the mortal in a universe full of immortals, knowledge can level the playing field.

The curator was Professor Johann Olafssen, a bear of a man with pale skin, blonde hair, ice blue eyes and an accent that was exactly what you would expect from someone hailing from the far-flung reaches of the Upper West Side of New York City. You kept expecting to hear something from him like out of the Swedish Chef. When he talked, though, he used the word "fuck" like a maestro, pronouncing it loud and proud like a New Yorker should: "Fawk!" Seriously, Joe Pesci could have taken lessons from him. I had last been to the museum a year prior, actually. The professor had been a bit of help during a personal matter, and him being an Egyptologist had made things, maybe not easier, but better for all concerned. I knew he was a workaholic and would still be at the museum until at least midnight. That gave me time, but I didn't want to dawdle.

If you've never been to the Norfolk waterfront,

you're missing out. With there almost always being a ship out there, whether wind-, diesel- or nuclear-powered, it would always set an incredible backdrop for any mood. Add in the restaurants, the small boat tours around the water, the concerts that would play on any given night, and you had reasons for the multiple five-star hotels that permeated the area. There were the museums, the aquarium, the library and of course the university, all within five miles of one hell of a beautiful view of the water. It was near perfect.

Of course, that was if you didn't know about the almost-successful attempt to raise a sea monster to lay waste to the east coast four years ago. Or the mer-creatures who lived in the deep part of the Chesapeake Bay, occasionally getting "hired" to do either some acting for the Aquatic Festival in the summers or salvage work by a certain detective who would be looking for stuff that got thrown in the water. Or the opening to hidden paths to other realms used by the gods and their designated ilk, located in a dark deserted corner on the first level of the parking garage at MacArthur Mall. Or that at any given time during the night, creatures and beings from legend would venture out into the crowds, blending into the crowds, sometimes mating with mortals, other times feeding on them.

You think that's bad, though, you should hear about New York; alligators in the sewers are the least of your worries.

All these things separately wouldn't really concern me. I mean, I've been dealing with the weirdness and the craziness that came along with being a private detective for years, and I have seen stuff that people wouldn't believe, and that's before adding in deities, half-deities, angels, demons, demigods and dragons. We mortals are a strange lot already; Don't believe me? Check YouTube. Add in beings who have tremendous colossal power with an itty bitty attention span and that's a recipe for disaster.

That's just one thing at a time, though. Put all these events and critters together, and you had a definite problem. I couldn't stop the feeling that things were changing, and my life would get more complicated. Even with my in-between status, I wasn't immortal, and I was really the only one who could do anything about it, whatever "it" might actually be.

I was sitting in a parking garage pondering all this. Part of being a detective is looking for patterns, and with all that was going on in the world that Larry and others had told me, and the things I had seen for myself... I didn't want to really think about the possibilities. While I always hated not enough information, there was also such a thing as too much information, and I hadn't really had enough time to sit down and sort it out.

I chided myself for borrowing trouble. There was a godly killer out there, and a mortal pulling his strings. There were more important things for me to do than sit in my car five minutes from a museum and ponder my navel.

As I headed down Waterside Drive, I took a deep breath of the evening air. The weather was turning cold, and I felt the wind bite through my clothes, making me shiver. It was going to be a cold winter, and had been a brisk autumn already. The water was pulling away any heat the breeze might have had, making my breath show and burning my lungs a bit. People walked by, paying only enough attention to not bump into me. I wasn't paying the crowd much mind; they were mostly harmless.

It was the guy in the dark coat that caught my attention.

He was about thirty feet behind me, keeping to groups to try and break up the line of sight. I wasn't getting a dangerous vibe from him, at least not dangerous to me. He was definitely on the prowl for someone, though, and I had caught his interest. Not a good thing, as I knew I was probably already on a radar I didn't want. Things would get dicey quickly if I didn't pay attention.

I made it to the museum with no problem, which told me my shadow wanted me to get there. Whether he wanted me to come out was an entirely different story. While in the entrance, I sent a quick text with a description to a friend, just in case. Once I had put my phone back in my coat, I nodded to the guard in greeting, motioning her not to get up. She smiled back before going back to her magazine. Always be nice to guards, kids. You never know when you might need a hand.

I walked through the nearly empty museum, hearing my footsteps echo off the walls. I could find my way through the whole place blindfolded, but I kept my eyes wide open so I could enjoy the exhibits, especially the new ones that had opened over the last week. I had been slacking on checking the new displays out, so I took an extra couple of minutes to take a gander. It was always nice to be able to look back on history and see where the world had been, since that was a good way to see where the world was going. Besides, it's not like Jiao was going to get any less dead.

My destination was the administrative offices in the rear of the museum. Professor Olafssen had the largest office, which meant it was packed even more with exhibits and papers and folders and whatever else might have found its way into the museum that might not yet have a home. While it was the largest, it was also way in the back, like as far back as possible and still be in the building. Not the easiest place to get to, but it allowed a bit of privacy.

When I made it to the back office, I saw a sign on the glass door with three simple words: "So long, suckers!" I got closer to confirm it was the professor's handwriting. Not only that, but the door was locked. To put the cherry on top, his name was removed from the glass; I could just see the outlines from the paint. In a bit of desperation, I jiggled the doorknob. It didn't turn so much as a hair, which brought a curse to my lips. That put rather a crimp on the evening, and my finding out anything about these coins.

As I stood there, pondering my next move, I heard a footstep. It was quiet, not too loud, and I only heard a single step. I smiled and said, still looking at the door, "I sent that text fifteen minutes ago."

"*Oui*, you did, Thomas," Luc Bertrand

answered, "but you neglected to mention his friend."

I turned to the Frenchman, nodding respectfully. "Hey, your people are big and grown and need the practice, right?"

"*D'accord*," Luc said, the slight smile on his face. I hadn't spoken to Luc Bertrand in awhile, mostly as our paths don't cross often. He moved in circles of society that I would likely never see, trading favors and information and lives with people who made nations move. Luc was a little shorter than me, a lot thinner, but I knew behind those ice-blue eyes was a mind that held more secrets and knowledge than almost any government intelligence agency. He kept his blond hair short, almost to the scalp. That night, he was dressed down, apparently, wearing a black and red track suit with a brown leather coat. I must have caught him on an off-night. After all, it wasn't often I saw the casual look on the leader of the Assassins' Guild of the east coast.

"So where are they?" I asked as we headed back to the main entrance. The professor was a dead end; I needed answers and I wasn't getting them there.

"The one you described is in hand. Apprentice Marisol is retrieving the other momentarily."

"Marisol?"

"Thomas, my order has been equal opportunity for as long as it has existed," Luc chuckled as we walked past a display of the Knights Templar. "*Des morceaux de merde*," he muttered, then spit. "Who puts such garbage on display?"

I laughed. "I doubt they put that there just to mess with you, man."

"Knowing the Templar, they would, *mon frere*." Luc shrugged as we made our way to the entrance. "It matters not. This is the first I've seen of the Templar in months." A vulpine grin formed. "Perhaps it is good they come; my apprentices need the practice."

Shaking my head, I said, "I don't need to know, Luc." I held the door open for him, nodding at the guard as I saw Luc drop her a wink. Her arms crossed over her chest in salute, and I saw her left ring finger.

Or lack thereof. Luc really does know where to put his people.

"Where don't you have people?" I asked.

"Heaven and Hell, *mon frere*," came the answer. "Once they die, they are free." Luc led me out to the cold, pulling his coat closed. He wouldn't have done that if it weren't safe. We made our way in short order to the nearby parking garage, specifically to a darkened section that had been closed off for repairs to the lights. I still don't know how Luc can get things done like that, but it was nice to know he could.

Frightening as all hell, too.

When we made it to the dark, I saw three people standing around a kneeling figure. The three were apprentices, but their faces were covered. I had a vague clue as to their identities, but this wasn't a social call, and I respected their privacy. Their clothes were perfectly nondescript, like something you'd see at your local outlet store, just out of style, exactly like everyone else's clothes, would help them blend into the crowd. The similar colors and styles, especially the hoods, were eerie, especially with the fact the three kept their faces hidden and they were all the same height and build.

That brought my gaze to the young man on his knees in the middle. From what I could tell, he was Asian, wearing a five hundred dollar sportcoat. The coat was being used to immobilize his arms, ruining it and exposing a silk shirt to the cold. I could see his feet were shoeless, and his ankles were crossed as he knelt. His hair was mussed, the grease or gel that he used to keep it in shape holding the damage done. There were blood flecks on his shirt, the source likely his lip, which was swollen. He knelt mute, probably wondering just how badly he was screwed.

The answer, as I was about to explain to him, was badly.

"Has he said anything?" I asked.

The assassin in the middle shook his head slightly.

"A shame." I hunkered down in front of the prisoner, who regarded me with a cold flat gaze. That dangerous feeling was now on me, and likely this guy would try to kill me if he could. Oh well, it wasn't like I didn't have enough to do. "Who sent you?" He still said nothing. "Listen, I'm sorry you got roughed up a bit, and I'm sure these three gentlemen are very sorry for that too. Aren't you?" I looked up at them, with silence being my only response.

"Actually, Thomas," Luc spoke up, "Marisol

did that. She was working lead on this call."

"Ah," I smiled. "You're pissed that a girl beat you up? That you got unmanned by a woman?" There was a spark of hatred in that look now. Not the cold-hearted killer type, apparently. "Don't feel bad; it happens all the time. I don't really care what you did, what you do or where you go after tonight. I just want to know who sent you." I might as well have been talking to a wall.

Okay. New plan.

"Luc, where's the other guy?" I looked up at the Frenchman but kept an eye on my new friend.

"He should be along shortly. Marisol does not fail."

There was a flash of fear. Very short, but I could see it. "So you can turn this guy into paste." It wasn't a question.

"You might want to step back."

I smiled again at the prisoner. "Now, I don't much condone torture, pal. Truth be told, I find it sub-human and counter-productive. I know all it gets you is someone saying whatever it takes to get the pain to stop." I shrugged. "That's why my friends here are going to make it relatively quick. Not painless," I clarified, "but relatively quick."

In spite of the cold, there was a sheen of sweat forming on his lips.

"Look, I don't much like being followed, so you tell me what I want to know, you might walk out of here. Otherwise, I can't vouch for your safety. My friends are very protective, and as you can see, very capable. Your choice."

Luc cleared his throat behind me. I turned

around and walked to him. "What's up?" I asked.

"It appears we have a problem."

I sighed. "I love problems. What is it?"

"This one's partner is no longer available." Luc's voice was more hesitant than I had heard it in quite awhile.

"Not available?" I raised an eyebrow. "How so?"

Luc gestured to the smaller assassin next to him. "I nearly had him," she said. Her voice was a bit unsteady, but controlled. "He had turned down an alley while I was above him. I looked away for a second, then looked back as he cried out.

"He was surrounded by several black dogs, all of them with red eyes. They tore him apart in a few seconds. Never have I seen anything like it." She shivered from the remembering; I didn't have to see her face to know she was scared.

"Good thing you didn't stick around, Marisol," I said. "That was a pack from the Wild Hunt. They don't usually come out this late in the winter." When Luc gestured for me to elaborate, I said, "Basically, you're talking about a group of immortal dogs hunting down someone or something, destroying anything that actively gets in their way. The leader of the Hunt is usually after someone in particular, but doesn't worry much about collateral damage. You, young lady," I said to Marisol, "were lucky. I take it you didn't try to stop them from tearing this guy apart?" She shook her hooded head. "Very smart. The Hunt doesn't cotton to others getting between them and their prey."

"Is this something with which I should be

concerned, Thomas?" Luc was protective of both his turf and his people.

I shook my head emphatically. "The Hunt only cares about those in their way. Your apprentice did the right thing."

Luc smiled. "*Bien*. So that just leaves us with this." He indicated the prisoner with a disdainful nod.

"Seems your partner won't be joining us after all, Chuckles," I said, turning around to the mute prisoner. The fear was gone, dammit, and in its place was a smugness I didn't care for much. "I imagine you think this means you're safe, since I wouldn't dream of hurting you for fear of not getting the information I needed, right?" I shrugged. "You're forgetting one thing: Your boss will send others. Now that my friends in the Guild know someone is looking for me, they can trace what's left of you to whoever is above you. Bottom line, my friend?

"I don't need you. I can wait for the next few idiots. I'm sure they'll be much more pliable, once they see what the Assassin's Guild does to you. Have a nice life. What's left of it, anyway." I turned away, and caught the look of fear again. "Luc, he's all yours."

The master assassin reached into his coat and removed a thin stiletto, almost an over-long needle. "You know it is nothing personal, *non*?" Luc said to the prisoner. "I do this out of necessity." Luc took a step forward, out of my sight. "It is said the first cut is the deepest; I disagree. It is, however, the most telling. Shall we begin?"

I got about five steps away before I heard in clear English "Okay, I'll talk!" That was three steps farther than I thought I'd get. I guess I need to work on my fearsome aspect.

When I turned around, I saw that Luc hadn't even touched him. Hadn't even laid finger to flesh, as it were. They just aren't making henchmen like they used to. "So start talking. Who sent you?"

"General Wu Zhe Hou! He wanted us to find you!"

I got close to him again, squatting down. "Okay, so this general wanted to find me. I'm in the book."

"He said he had to know if you were clean!" The shouting was already getting on my nerves, and from what I could tell, Luc's. I closed my eyes, shook my head, then looked up at Luc. He replied with a near-imperceptible nod.

The assassin's blade made another appearance, like magic, at the prisoner's jawline. "Speak loudly again, and you will need pen and paper to communicate your thoughts, *me comprenez*?" Though I doubted Chuckles understood French, he certainly got the message.

"Sorry, I'm sorry," the poor bastard sniffled. I have no idea what kind of look Luc had on his face once I turned away, but it must have been something on the order of the nine hells itself.

"You got a name?" I asked, trying to keep the words flowing.

"Parker," he said. "Parker Chou."

"Well, Parker Chou, you're going to go back to your boss, you're going to let him know that I'm clean, whatever the hell that's supposed to mean, and that my office opens around nine tomorrow morning. You're also going to tell him that you're going to be there with him, so no killing the messenger." I thought I saw some relief on his face, which he didn't deserve, but I was in a charitable mood. "Now get the fuck out of here, before I change my mind and let these good people do whatever they want to you."

Parker took off like all the demons of the nine hells were after him, which probably wasn't far from the truth as far as he was concerned. I had bigger problems, namely the exact question I asked Luc as soon as Parker was out of sight:

"Who the hell is General Wu Zhe Hou?"

Luc quirked a smile before making some kind of gesture with his right hand. Like ghosts, his apprentices vanished, as if they had never been. That kind of skill always scared the crap out of me. "He is known to me, if only by reputation," Luc said. He had turned away from me to look out over the parking garage's open spaces. "If the rumors are true, and I do not think they are not, he was a vicious man, calculating and cruel. There are stories that he was sent to North Korea when he was in his early thirties by the Chinese high command." We began walking toward my car, which was two levels above us. I could hear my shoes on the pavement, while Luc made no sound at all. I really had to learn how to do that.

"No shit? What did he do wrong?"

Luc shook his head. "Nothing. He was sent to train the secret police there, and the women agents, or songbirds as they were called. The songbirds were always effective, and they were trained quite well. Apparently, Dear Leader thought his people could learn something from their Chinese benefactors." The assassin's voice dropped fifty degrees. "He was right. Then-Major Hou was promoted for his work in training, all of which lead to an even more efficient purge in the Koreas."

"How many?" I asked.

"Seventeen deep-cover agents killed with twice that number forced to flee. We lost more than just people in those months. We called him *La Mort Jaune.*"

The Yellow Death, I mentally translated. "I'm sorry, man," I said. I couldn't imagine what Luc had gone through.

A mirthless laugh came from the Frenchman. "Don't be. The Order has a long memory, and after time, our reach returns, and one bird deserves another." I almost asked the obvious question, but a shake of Luc's head quieted me. "The general eluded us, though; China is a world unto itself. Though the Order has made inroads over the last few centuries, this 'communist' phase has put a crimp on our plans, and when everyone is watching everyone else, it is nearly impossible to act in secret."

"Hence why you couldn't find him."

"Indeed. He disappeared into the bureaucracy of the Chinese government and emerged a newly minted general and in charge of *Dieu* knew what. We weren't even sure he was still alive until a few years ago."

"And now he's wanting to talk to me." We stopped as I reached the Beauty. "I really don't like this."

"Thomas," Luc said, his voice low, "I know of my oath to you regarding the Order's operations here. I ask for an exception."

I knew this was coming the moment I heard Luc start talking about the bad old days. "Why?"

"Other than the fact that he's worth less than the scum on a shoe that has trod through a sewer? He was responsible for the deaths of more than a dozen of my Order, and *Dieu* knows how many innocents." Luc looked at me imploringly. "I cannot let their deaths go unavenged."

"No." The word was out of my mouth before I could pull it back. Luc's visage went dark, like the entrance to Hell itself. His eyes darkened except for pinpricks of bright red in the center of them, the lips tightening into a snarl. That must have been what Parker Chou saw. "Not yet, anyway. I might need some information from him about the case I'm on right now. Give me a week or so, then you can tear him apart; I won't care. Just do it elsewhere, okay?"

The assassin took a deep breath to steady himself. "As you wish. One week." Luc opened my car door, which I could have sworn I had locked. Show-off. "I understand your need for information, Thomas, and I would not ask for this dispensation otherwise, but---"

"It's a matter of honor, Luc. I get it, believe me." I laughed. "That's pretty much the only reason I'm still on this case." I smiled. "Once I'm done, he's all yours."

Luc smiled back. "I will hold you to that, my friend. Go on home. It's late, and you have an appointment tomorrow, *n'est pas?*"

"I need a godsdamned social secretary at this rate," I grumbled as I climbed into the Beauty. "I'll talk to you soon."

"Thomas, be careful with this man," Luc warned. "General Hou is not one with whom you should trust or trifle. He is an evil man, and will likely try to kill you."

I shrugged. "Wouldn't be the first time someone's tried."

Luc shut the door firmly, then waited for me to roll the window down. "Let us hope, then, that he is not the first to succeed."

Chapter Six

Once I got back to Hampton, I sent a message to Susana to let her know I was at the office and I was still looking into a few matters about Jiao's death, especially as far as my side of the weirdness went. It was mostly just to allay her worries that I had done something stupid during the night, which I had been known to do once or twice a week. I kicked my shoes off and crawled into bed, not even bothering with getting undressed the rest of the way. The last thing I remember before passing out was telling Larry to wake me if anything strange happened during the night.

Well, stranger than normal.

The next thing I knew, there was light coming through the window, and it seemed to have found the exact perfect angle to shine in my eyes. I took stock of the place, mostly just to try and bring myself conscious. My bedroom was functional, little more than that. A simple twin bed, dresser and nightstand were the only pieces of furniture, while an overhead fan also provided light from two of the three bulbs. Light brown thin carpet was on the floor, which at least kept my feet from freezing too much during the winter months. It wasn't much, but it was home. While the place wasn't zoned for residential use, I had made a deal with the landlord, Mr. Martoukas, for some work I had done for him.

I had tangled in the sheets somehow, and Larry was standing over me with an expectant look.

"It is morning, Thomas."

I think I grumbled a "No shit" to him as I

untangled myself, managing not to tear anything or fall out of bed. I'm rarely at my best before ten in the morning, and looking at the clock, it was about ten after nine. I managed to clear my throat and ask "The hell did you wake me up?"

"You have company," Larry answered. "They do not look happy."

"How many?"

"Three Chinese gentlemen. One elderly, two younger, one of the younger looks scared out of his mind. All three are dressed quite well, Armani for the lot, with Gucci shoes and I believe the unafraid one has a knife in his right sleeve. The scared one appears to be carrying a pistol, though his coat is closed. The elderly gentleman is almost a stereotype out of the movies, with a balding pate, Fu Manchu mustache and goatee, and short hair on the sides. He does not appear to be armed, though I would not say it is out of the realm of possibility that his cane is a weapon." Larry smiled a bit. "Friends of yours?"

I yawned, my jaw creaking from the action. "Hell no. Probably here to cause trouble." I heaved myself to my feet with a grunt, stretching until I heard a few pops from my back and shoulders. "Don't I have a rule about more than one case at a time?"

"Not that I know of, Thomas." Larry went to the closed bedroom door and peeked through the wood. When he pulled himself back, he shook his head. "They have not moved."

"I locked the door, right?"

"They seem to have remedied that situation."

I sighed deeply. That's how they wanted to play

it, eh? Fine. I tore open the door and went to walk right past the three men, the younger two seemingly surprised by the sudden door opening. The oldest of the three sat between the young ones, one of whom was Parker Chou. I made a beeline for the fridge, which wasn't in my bedroom mainly due to there being no room. Before I had made it a quarter of the way, the young one that wasn't Parker stepped in front of me to block my path.

Not the best way to get on my good side.

"Mr. Statford," he said in crisp English, which didn't surprise me much, "you are late in opening your office for the General."

"And you are an asshole blocking me from my caffeine," I retorted. "Move it or you lose teeth."

He drew back as if I had waved dog crap under his nose. "How dare you speak in such a manner!"

"Easy. You're in my office." As he tried to talk again, I made a nonsense noise to shut him up. It took three times before he stopped talking. "Good. Move."

As he moved aside, I walked past him and waved at Parker, who still looked as if I was going to eviscerate him. He looked down in shame and said nothing. I shrugged and made my way to the source of my power: Mountain Dew. I pulled the fridge open and pulled out a bottle, twisting the cap, then flicking it into the garbage. I was about to take a drink when I felt a hand descending on my shoulder. "Pal, I don't give a shit who you are, but if you don't get your hand off of me, you will draw back a bloody stump." The hand jerked away as if from a fire, and I walked to my desk and took a seat in my chair. "I'm not completely awake yet, so if you'll give me two minutes, I'll be happy to listen to whatever it is you have to say before I decide if I want to call the cops on three guys breaking into my office." I kicked my bare feet up on the desk and took a drink, the cold soda with life-giving caffeine starting my brain working. I checked the clock.

"How dare you speak to the general in such a manner!" The younger one, whom I named Chip in my head, roared. To be fair, it was a pretty impressive roar. He was average height and build, with the usual dark hair and round face a Chinese man would have. His eyes were aglow with rage, though, which I admit made me somewhat giddy. Why yes, I can be a bit of an asshole just after waking up. "You do not know your place, ignorant peasant. That you are not weeping blood from a dozen wounds by now is only because of the General's kindness! You are unworthy of being in his presence, let alone have his attention! You should feel privileged that he even acknowledges your existence, let alone come into the disgusting pit of filth that you call a place of business!"

I sighed and took another drink. He had a very commanding voice, and his diction was excellent. Ninety.

"Do you not know just who this is? He is a man who left behind his entire life to come to this dirty country! He has provided opportunity for so many, and all you can do is sit there with your bottle of piss and look like a stupid American!" I wondered what Susana was doing. Probably sleeping, still. It was her day off, and she had most likely worked late the night before. At least I hadn't had much to do with that. "You should feel thankful I do not teach you the manners you sorely lack, for it is only by the General's forgiveness that I do not slit your throat."

Sixty. Maybe I would go for Thai food at lunch. It had been awhile since I had had really good Thai food.

Chip slammed his hands down on the desk, threatening to topple two very precarious piles of paper that I had to file eventually. "How can you just sit there? Are you as stupid as the rest of this country? Do you not understand the words I use? Are they too advanced for you? Should I speak in the grunts that you are used to hearing? Would that be more to your liking?"

Thirty. I took a long swig and closed my eyes.

"This is with what my country wants to do business? Some slack-witted fool who fills his body with poison and treats his betters with such disrespect? You are the poorest excuse for a human being that I have ever had the misfortune of seeing. You are nothing more than excrement that I would scrape off my shoe!"

Zero.

"Ah, much better," I said, smiling broadly. "So what can I do for you gentlemen?"

That seemed to throw Chip off, but it did get Parker to smother a laugh, and I heard Larry laugh long and hard. The old man sat there, seemingly carved from wood, but I thought I saw a minute curl of a smile. Chip went right back laying into me. "You *biao zi yang de*!" He turned to the old man who was sitting on his right and spoke in quiet Chinese.

I gave a quick glance to Larry, who said, "He called you a son of a whore, and is now asking the older gentleman if he should go get the children in the pictures to make you more polite."

"You go near them," I growled, putting my feet on the floor, "or even think about going near them, there isn't a god or demon new or ancient that will keep me from fucking ending you."

Apparently, those were fighting words.

I saw Chip twitch his right arm and a piece of metal slide out of his sleeve. Ducking down and to my left, I dodged his initial strike, grabbing his arm with my hands. With no fuss or fanfare, I brought the wrist down on the edge of my desk. Bone lost against wood with a sickening crack, and the blade fell from useless fingers. My right hand grabbed the knife in mid-air by the handle, reversed it, and stabbed it through the fabric of his coat. The wavy blade was about eight inches long, and I had just embedded an inch of it into the top of my desk. As he started to cry out and reach for the knife, I brought my fist down hard on the back of his head, making his nose bounce on the hard wood. My left hand grabbed his hair and forced his face down while my right hand brought out my Beretta and pushed it against his temple.

"Now, as I was saying," I said, my words coming out through clenched teeth, "what can I do for you gentlemen?"

Parker was barely out of his seat, so fast it had happened. His mouth was open, whether to say something or other was irrelevant. I noticed his hand hadn't gone to his coat, which was still closed. The left armpit had a bulge that was vaguely gun-like. It seemed to me Parker wasn't a mook so much as a gofer. The gun probably wasn't even loaded, and he made no move for it regardless. He may have been a gofer, but he was a smart gofer.

The old man still sat like a stone. Not moving. Just regarding me with a blank stare that seemed to weigh everything without pity. It was a bit unnerving, but I'd seen worse. His eyes flicked almost imperceptibly from me to Chip, who had begun screaming in Chinese to whoever would listen and struggling. Chip's words cut off like a switch when I pulled the hammer back and tapped his cheekbone with the barrel, which was fine with me; the yelling was getting too much.

"I take it you wanted to see me?" I said to the old man. To Chip, I said, "I'm going to let you go. We have an understanding?" He nodded, pure hatred on his face. "Good." I sat back in my chair, keeping the gun out just in case. Chip pulled his knife out, and I saw the bruise forming on his left cheekbone, along with the blood coming out of his nose from the initial impact on the desk. "You can leave the knife there," I commanded with a smile.

Without a word, he let it thump onto the wood and paper, holding my gaze like a viper. Holding his broken wrist gently, he moved to leave, and was stopped by the old man's hand coming up, then gesturing at a chair. I almost felt sorry for the guy as he sat, cradling his right arm, the agony he had to be feeling and knowing he couldn't leave just yet plain on his face. I almost felt sorry for him.

Almost.

"Mr. Statford," the old man began, his accent threading in and out of his words, "I apologize for my son's actions. He is young and prideful and protective of his elders."

"He does seem to need a lesson in manners," I said as I leaned back. Amazing what a little caffeine can do. "Your man there," I indicated Parker, who hadn't said a word yet, "said you needed to see me, and that you wanted to make sure I was 'clean', wasn't it, Parky?" The younger man nodded quickly. "So whatever that means, I guess I am, so you want to explain what I can do for you?"

"Straight to the point," the elderly man said approvingly. "I wish you to find my granddaughter."

"Your granddaughter?" I replied dumbly. "She's missing? Haven't you tried the police? They're more up on missing persons than I am."

"The police would not be able to find the granddaughter of General Wu Zhe Hou, Mr. Statford." The general sighed deeply. "I doubt anyone could."

"So why come to me?"

"You came highly recommended."

"If you say by Ehr-Lang, I will be very depressed." I smiled as I said it, but the general didn't seem to be in a laughing mood.

"Who referred me is immaterial, Mr. Statford," he said, his voice quavering slightly. "That you can find her is not."

I shrugged; no need to get into a pissing contest

with this guy. After all, I had just broken his son's wrist. "Okay, so what have you got to help me find her?"

"Her name is Xu Bai Rong. She was my only granddaughter." For just a moment, his iron control seemed to slip as a tear fell down his cheek. "I have been looking for her for over three years, I have traced her here, and I am told that you are the one who will find her."

"General Hou, while I find your faith in me flattering, I'm still not sure why you haven't contacted the cops, especially since she's been missing for years."

The old man was implacable. "Mr. Statford, you will find my granddaughter, and you will not involve the police." I started to protest, then he said, "For this, I will pay you two hundred thousand American dollars." He paused, then added, "Cash."

Now, before you folks start thinking I'm just in the business of making money, you'd be wrong. Being a private detective pays less than you'd expect. In fact, most PIs who get into the business end up either going the "private security" route in a year or less because they won't compromise their scruples, or they compromise their scruples, make a lot of money and either get out or get killed for one too many shady deals. That I had a special clientele gave me a little bit of an edge, but not much. I had bills like everyone else, which were sometimes hard to pay thanks to my scruples. So it wasn't that we were talking about money that got me interested.

It was that we were talking about a shitload of money.

"Okay, I have a name," I said. "How about a picture? Last known address? Friends? Anything that might narrow things down?"

The general smiled slightly. "It is good to know that there are still people who are true in this world, Mr. Statford. My associate will give you the pertinent information." General Hou gave a short command in Chinese, which had Parker jump up and unbutton his coat. I would have raised my weapon but he was reaching with his left hand, so unless he was a lot more flexible than I gave him credit for, I was okay. Out came a thumb drive, which was placed rather delicately on the desk. Parker was showing brains, which I definitely appreciated. "On that device is everything you need to know about how to find her, Mr. Statford."

"That's it?" I shrugged. Hell, if he already had the information, I could wrap this one up pretty quickly if I wanted. Even though I still had no clue as to where to find my former client's sister, I figured she was probably safe for the moment. If she wasn't, well, there wasn't much I could do about it anyway, probably.

"That should be sufficient, Mr. Statford. We shall be in touch." The old man stood slowly, regally, not seeming to place any weight on his cane. Two crisp commands in Chinese and Parker and Chip followed him, though the latter gave me a long nasty look as he nursed his broken wrist. My return gaze was mild. I knew the look, having seen it before a thousand times on a thousand different gods and humans. He was a bully, he was used to doing the hurting, and he knew he had just gotten his ass beaten. I also could tell that he would never follow through on his threats against me and mine. Once bullies get a taste of their own medicine, they rarely push their luck. Still, I felt a huge weight lift from me as they finally got out of sight.

"Well, that was enjoyable," Larry mused.

"Says you, ya bastard," I groused. "My desk has a knife wound in it."

"It is but a scratch."

"A scratch? A godsdamned knife went through it!"

A twitch of Larry's mouth betrayed the humor. "It has had worse."

I laughed as I finally got the reference. "Come along, Patsy," I said as Arthurian as possible. I went to my room and finished dressing, getting more and more sure that this was my second bad idea in as many days. Oh well, it could always have been worse.

You know, one of these days, I'm going to stop myself from even thinking of those words, because not only could it get worse; it would get worse.

Now, I won't say I'm the sharpest knife in the drawer, but I do know when I'm getting fed a line of crap. I was driving to meet up with Susana for the aftermath of the previous night, and I wanted to make sure I had everything straight in my head before I got there. The general had been mostly straight with me, but I expect he knew I was very aware of his past. The "lost granddaughter" was likely a smokescreen for something else, but I couldn't think of what. I'd put it on the back burner for a day, as I had other things on my mind, and I hadn't even looked at the thumb drive yet.

Besides, I was still sore about the hole in my desk. He could wait.

Susana wanted to let me know what had been found, in case it might help my case. Granted, I didn't even have much of a case; at this point, it was just curiosity and the desire to find out who could pull off something so huge. Most wouldn't think that being able to pull a deity's strings is a big deal, as they either only believe in their own personal god or don't believe at all. I was a believer by circumstance, but I didn't have the luxury of choosing who I believed in. My friend Father Martin had once told me it didn't matter what I believed in, as long as I believed. There's not much need for philosophy when you constantly rub shoulders with the eternal. When the answers to life, the universe and everything are at your beck and call, it's actually not that interesting, especially as the answers usually boil down to "We did it because we thought it would be cool."

I pulled into the parking lot where Susana had her apartment. I had been spending more and more time over at her place the last few months, so I tossed the visitor badge onto my dashboard. No need to get towed quite yet. Susana had gotten it for me several weeks prior, but I still got a bit of a thrill using it. Yeah, it's silly, but hey, with all she and I had been through, it was nice to know she still wanted me around, even when I was a complete chowderhead.

She pulled the door open before I knocked.

"About time you came over." Susana looked tired, worn out and like she had rolled out of bed five minutes before she opened the door. Her hair was in disarray, she wasn't wearing makeup and she was wearing the Han Shot First t-shirt I had gotten her for Christmas for the second time in a week.

"Hi, babe," I smiled. "You look great."

"You're a shitty liar. Come on in," she said, letting me pass the threshold. As she closed the door, I pulled her close. "Get offa me, gringo," Susana purred with no real malice. "I haven't even brushed my teeth yet."

The apartment itself hadn't changed much in the last few days since I had been over, even given Susana's habit of switching around furniture on a random basis. She had a first floor flat, which gave her a patio with a sliding glass door leading outside to a grassy area that kids would play in during the warmer months or during the infrequent snowfalls in the winter. Susana had kept the couch against the western wall where the door was, with a loveseat on the opposite wall. There were throw rugs and pillows everywhere, a glass coffee table covered in magazines and folders, a flatscreen TV where she watched her reality shows that were about as real as an honest politician, and a couple of bookcases filled half with books and keepsakes. Given pride of place was a small ceramic plate, cracks spiderwebbing from the center, the piece of lead embedded deep. I remembered the night I had given that to Susana all too well.

"Oh dear, whatever will I do?" I asked in mock concern. A quick peck on the cheek later, I sent

Larry out of the apartment with a nod. After the godslayer case, I took no chances. "So what did you find, darlin?" I asked as I sat on the couch, tossing my coat on a nearby chair.

She took a seat next to me and leaned on me, stifling a yawn. "Another one for the cold case file. Parkinson is pissed, but what's he going to do?" Susana flopped a hand at a manila folder on the coffee table. I decided to wait to take a look at it; she was getting comfortable as I put my arm around her. "Your girl was definitely dead, along with the two goons."

"I figured that."

"Well, what you might not have figured was we had a Chinese guy in our CSI." I groaned. "Yeah, it was bad. He kept his mouth shut until afterward." Another yawn, this one not stifled. "He came to me once the scene was secured, which was around four this morning."

"Ouch."

"Would have been later if Harley hadn't told Parkinson to wrap it up because we were all wasted." She was talking about resident medical examiner Harley Blackwater, a mutual friend and full-blooded Seneca Indian. "Harley was spooked, though."

"How could you tell?" I asked, stroking her hair.

"He took me aside and said that you'd probably need a lot of help on this one." She looked up sidelong at me. "He also said you needed to stop wearing those damned Chuck Taylors." Dammit. Harley was also the best tracker ever of all time; I should have known he would notice my having been there. "Anyway, he said that as near as he could tell, death was instantaneous, and he'd have the COD by noon, but wouldn't give it to me until one at the earliest, so I could get some sleep. His words." She stretched again, nearly punching me in the face. "So I did, and then some *pendejo* of a private dick called me to find out what happened. Well," she pointed at the folder, "there it is. Everything so far until Harley gets done with the autopsy."

I glanced again at the folder. "Not a hell of a lot there."

"There'd be more if said pendejo PI hadn't taken a couple of things from the scene."

Ouch. "Yeah, I know, but I couldn't risk someone getting hold of something very bad." I told her enough about the coins to convince her that taking it with me was the better idea. "I don't know if it's communicable like that, but I'd rather not take the chance."

"Parkinson would crucify you for that," Susana said, her voice slurring a bit as I began massaging her neck.

"Of course he would," I sighed as I worked at a knotted muscle. "I just need to be more careful, and I need to find out what the hell these coins do."

Susana looked up again at me. "What about that guy at the museum? Wouldn't he be able to help you?"

I shook my head. "Apparently, he won the lottery and told us all to piss off. Can't say I blame him; this place has gotten pretty strange the last few years."

"Well, that sucks." She curled up again against me, which was followed by a soft snore. What can I say? I love to keep my audience riveted. As I lifted her gently back to bed, I was amazed by how light she was, yet this same woman had taken down the Devil bare-handed. As I put the covers over her, I heard a throat clear behind me.

"What is it, Larry?" I whispered while leaving the room. She needed a lot more rest, and I wasn't about to let a one-sided conversation with my spectral partner wake her up.

"Perhaps we should head to Chinatown," he said, his own voice hushed, even though Susana couldn't hear him. "It is a little out of the way, however, it is unlikely anyone will be at the museum again, especially so soon after the professor's droll farewell."

I shook my head emphatically. "Oh hell no. I have no desire to go down there. Bad things happen to people who go poking around there."

"We may not have a choice." Larry paused, then said "We might be able to find out about the general's granddaughter, as I doubt you wish to return that money."

"I'll go only if I have to." I really didn't want to have to go to Chinatown. Too much risk for too little gain. "I haven't exhausted all my options yet."

"Speaking of options, are you going to turn the assassins loose on the general? I imagine they are quite anticipating the hunt."

I picked up my coat and slipped it on, not trusting myself to answer until I was ready. "Not yet," I decided. "Luc knows this is a delicate time, and his order has waited this long; they can wait another few days."

"So where does that leave you?"

"I need to find out where these coins come from," I said. "Priorities. Anyone who can order around a god needs to be taken out of the picture first. It sucks for the general, but I'm on a bit more of a time crunch."

"There is a possibility, Thomas." Larry pursed his lips in thought, then said, "The timing is rather suspect, is it not?"

"What's that?"

"These coins show up, your client with the salable morals shows up, then shows up dead, and this general comes looking for his granddaughter."

I sat back and thought it through. "The General is Jiao's grandfather? That could make sense, considering he said the cops would never find her, and she did have an uncanny ability to get out of trouble. It would also make this a very easy case. I deserve one or two of those every ice age, right?" I laughed.

"Perhaps, Thomas, though I am not as convinced of his paternal nature. He is not what I would call a very warm and caring man." Larry began to pace, which was unnerving from both the silence and the idea that a spirit would show such nervousness.

Larry had hit it on the head. This guy didn't give a damn about finding his granddaughter. Even though I wasn't an expert on how different cultures treated their kids, I expected some kind of warmth from the relative of a missing child. He might have been talking more about a long lost pet rather than his blood. Besides, Jiao was too old to be his granddaughter. No, there was something deeper here, and I was starting to get the idea that I would find out what it was just before it smacked me in the face and called me an asshole.

"Come on, Larry," I said, keeping my voice down as I left Susana's apartment. "We'll try the museum one more time; they have to have at least a temporary curator."

He glided beside me, keeping pace as I unlocked the Beauty. "You do know the definition of insanity, do you not, Thomas?"

I chuckled. "Most certainly. However, my fine feathered friend, I'm going during daylight hours, when there's likely to actually be someone there. It's not like the same shit is going to happen to the same guy twice."

Okay, you can stop laughing any time now.

Chapter Seven

"I did find a bit about those coins while you were taking care of Susana," Larry said. "They seem to have a rather storied and sordid history."

A wrecker passed by on my right as I was sitting in the lunch rush, about two miles worth of cars between me and the opening of the Hampton Roads Bridge Tunnel. Likely, I could have walked to Norfolk and made it faster. The cold weather persisted, making my heater work overtime as I tried to stay warm. Thankfully, no snow had yet fallen, but with the way the clouds looked, it was going to happen sooner rather than later. "You aren't just saying this to pass the time and keep me from bitching about the traffic?"

"Most definitely, but at the least, it will be educational." Larry had his sardonic smile on, which meant that this would be more than just something to show off his knowledge.

"Okay, spill. What are they?"

Larry crossed his legs in the passenger seat of the Beauty, disconcerting me as always when his legs went through the dashboard. I figured I would retire once that got to be commonplace to me. "As I earlier surmised, they are ancient, dating back to the first emperor."

"Of China?" I whistled.

"No, Thomas, of the Upper West Side," Larry gave me a baleful glare. "Of course, China. I honestly do not know why I bother trying to enlighten you."

I laughed. "Lighten up."

"This is serious business, Thomas, and these are very dangerous artifacts," the spirit admonished. When I looked properly chastened, Larry continued. "Good. Now, as I was saying, these were created in the time of the first emperor. Of China."

"Yeah, I get it, around the first emperors of China."

"No, Thomas, I mean the *first*." He accented the word so I would know what he meant.

I sighed as I scooted the Beauty forward a record-breaking six inches. "So let's pretend the closest I got to ancient Chinese history is the lunch menu at Golden Wok, and you tell me why these coins are so almighty important? My fun meter is about pegged, Larry."

"You have no sense of drama." Larry shot his cuffs and crossed his arms. "As I was saying, the first emperor of China, Qin Shihuang, was not all that popular back then. He was actually rather a right bastard to his people, and to those he attempted to conquer. He taught a group of them how to farm, and they revolted anyway. A pity, really.

"It was after the third attempt on his life that he became obsessed with the idea of living forever. Of course, this was not the only thing with which he became obsessed. Qin Shihuang was mad as a hatter, but he wanted to make sure that, if he did not survive the next try at assassination, that whoever did it and whoever was behind it would not be long for the world."

"Kind of a deadman's switch," I commented.

"Precisely." Larry smiled. "The emperor

commissioned the minting of six coins, which would be his way of making sure whoever was the architect of his demise met their own in the worst way possible. The cost to the emperor was very high." The spirit went quiet for a moment, and I looked over as I put my parking brake back on. "Exceptionally high, but when one is a paranoid lout with ideas of vengeance, perhaps cost is no object." When I raised my eyebrows in question, Larry said, "He had three of his sons and three of his daughters killed, their bones crushed and mixed with the gold, the coins themselves cooled in their blood."

"Charming."

"Undoubtedly. Now, the interesting part of this whole thing is that it actually worked. As you made note, the gods do not like to have artifacts lying around, and these artifacts in particular are rather troubling and trouble-making." Larry made a show of inhaling. "Qin Shihuang was a god to his people, and belief is the lifeblood of the gods, ergo the belief of his people was enough to infuse power into the coins."

Cars started moving in front of me, which was a good sign. "What kind of power?"

"Control."

"Control over the executioner of the gods?" I asked. "That's bad."

Larry tutted at my mistake. "Not quite, Thomas. The user of the coins gets control over one of the gods. Any one of them." My ethereal friend let that sink in. "A perfect example was when Qin Shihuang died before getting the elixir of immortality he craved."

"Murdered, I take it."

Larry chuckled. "You might just make it as a detective one day, Thomas. It was murder most foul, and of course, with his dying breath, the emperor sent one of his 'peers' to avenge his death. It did not end well."

I glanced over as I put the Beauty into fourth gear for the first time in an hour. "How not well?"

"Chang'e is the goddess of the moon, a truly lovely creature." I shrugged. "Because of her beauty, she drove the men who killed the emperor mad, bringing down the Qin Dynasty. Madness, or lunacy, if you will, was the way she did it, causing them to betray and kill each other."

"And I'll bet there were six of these people, and each died a rather horrible way." I didn't want to think about it; the Chinese as a people had existed as a civilization for nearly three thousand years and had likely forgotten more ways to kill people than most people knew nowadays.

"Mortals do have a bit of skill at discovering harsh things to end your lives, and you would win that bet."

"So you're saying it could have been any of them that showed up?"

"Yes. Be thankful it was not Gong Gong this time. It was less surgical."

I maneuvered around someone who decided that it was a good day to drive like a moron. "Who's Gong Gong?"

"A sea god. Not a terribly pleasant fellow, I assure you."

"How less surgical?"

"The Yellow River floods of 1887," Larry said, his voice tight. "September and October, to be exact. The river flooded to the point of claiming well over a million lives, as a conservative estimate."

"Gong Gong did that?"

"The same. From what tell I have heard, he got tired of waiting for the targets to show themselves and moved a few things around underground." Larry paused. "He was sanctioned for several decades for his actions."

I rolled my eyes. Kill a million people and get a slap on the wrist. For a god, being sanctioned is the equivalent of getting put in the corner for a time-out. We mere mortals may think a few decades is too long for a sentence, but for a god? A year is like a sneeze, and those decades Larry said are how long it takes to say gesundheit. "Yeah, probably a good idea we're just dealing with a pissed-off fire god."

"There is more than meets the eye here, Thomas," Larry said. "We are dealing with someone who thought it a good idea to take a chance for a random deity to kill six people. This is not something one trifles with unless one does not know the consequences..." The spirit trailed off.

"Or doesn't care." I finished. "The thought had occurred to me." And it scared the hell out of me, too.

I made it to the museum around noon after stopping for a bite to eat. While I was eating, I pondered the small thumb drive the General had given me. The story about his granddaughter didn't really hold much water, which kind of made things rather interesting in my mind, as my initial client had shuffled off this mortal coil in a rather fantastic way. Also, Larry was right: an officer of the People's Liberation Army, a general at that, had sought me out the very day after arguably one of the most powerful figures in Chinese organized crime had paid me a visit, only to get snuffed. Two very different people from very different walks of life go to the same gumshoe?

I'm a detective. I don't believe in coincidences.

Larry was back at Susana's, as I wanted him to keep an eye on her. I doubted anyone wanted to go after her, but when Triads, Communist Chinese intelligence generals and godly assassins are running around, I felt it prudent to keep a watch over my lady. I don't like to leave things to chance, and I always want to make sure that, no matter what, the people I love are taken care of.

As I threaded my way through the crowd, my eyes were constantly sweeping the streets, looking for anyone or anything out of the ordinary. I figured there wouldn't be much, as Parker Chou was probably keeping well clear of the place that nearly saw the end of his life, and I had passed whatever insane requirements the General had placed on me. That made my life rather easy, since I wouldn't have to worry about revenge from a certain broken-wristed tough guy, as the General had likely made messing with me and mine a capital offense.

Chip had been a problem, probably for both me and the old man. His son? Unlikely, I thought while dodging a small group of young-looking business-class people. The two looked absolutely nothing alike, and the deference a son would show for his father wasn't there. Chip acted more like a jilted heir-apparent than the son of the boss, and wasn't shy about showing it. That would be a big power struggle that I would be quite happy to miss.

A right turn, and my thoughts turned back to the night before at the hotel. It was hard to believe it had been less than a day since I had seen Jiao Shenjing walk into my office asking for help, and only a little less than eighteen hours since I had last seen her corpse on thick carpet, cooling to room temperature. She had been defiant to the last, shooting at an implacable god bent solely on her destruction, probably knowing she was going to die, but determined to spit back in the Grim Reaper's face. A hell of a woman, with a mile of guts, even if she was a scumbag.

Speaking of scumbags, that brought the General to mind. While he had been much more gentile than Jiao, he also probably had as much pull as she had, probably more. The guy most likely had enough underlings to find anyone he wanted, whenever he wanted. I probably could have asked him to find my third grade teacher, and that was nearly three decades past. The old man was likely playing a different game, but one that didn't really involve me except tangentially. Of course, that I had gotten his attention in the first place made me rather uncomfortable. That the old man had Luc's attention made me even more uncomfortable, especially with the obvious bad blood that the General probably didn't know about, or even worse didn't care. I had impressed the old man, though, at least enough that I was on his good side. So I strolled down Waterside Drive in the bright sun, the water to my left across a street with hundreds of people walking and driving all around me, watchful but confident that there was nothing I couldn't handle.

Of course, that's when I felt the bump against me, then the hard angled shape of a gun against my back, which just went to show I needed to start reading Batman comics again.

"Thomas Statford?" came the clipped accent in my left ear.

I looked around and saw how neatly I had been surrounded, without even noticing. Two of the business-type people who had passed me earlier flanked me, and as we walked, a youngish Asian man peeled himself off the wall ahead to my right and smiled at me crookedly before falling into step about four steps in front of me. My escorts to the sides were two arm-lengths away, which negated any chance of getting hold of one or the other. Both were Asian, and I guessed Chinese, and giving me a cold stare, looking very severe in their business attire. I hadn't gotten the chance to see the one behind me, but considering the very large barrel of a pistol was lodged securely against my third lumbar vertebra, it didn't much matter what the asshole looked like.

"Just keep walking, Statford," came the order from my ear. "We'll turn into the alley in a bit. You don't mind, do you?"

"Well, I did have to return some movies," I

said. "You know those late fees are a bitch."

No reaction from my wingmen to both sides, but I got a chuckle from the point man. Nothing emotional from behind me, but I pegged the voice as younger, shorter and very confident when it answered, "Perhaps you should refrain from getting things you can't afford to give back." As we approached the mouth of the alley, the point man went in while the four of us stopped. "It was very unfortunate you did not choose wisely," the mouthpiece said behind me. Not the average tough guy voice that would bend at the slightest form of resistance, but one with strength that would withstand whatever was thrown at it.

In other words, I was in trouble. What a refreshing change of pace.

The point man came back and said something in rapid-fire Chinese. The barrel of the gun jabbed me again, this time guiding me into the alleyway. My escorts were forced closer to me, but not close enough to grab. They weren't run-of-the-mill thugs; they knew their business, which in this case was making sure I would get my ass either beaten to a pulp, which was bad, or shot, which was worse. That they had taken me somewhere private didn't bode well for me, but considering they had taken the time to get me there instead of putting a bullet into me on the streets, it was a silver lining in a very dark cloud.

The alley itself was typical, about ten feet wide, dark and littered with dirt and waste. The entrance was brick, about fifteen feet in, where it opened up wide. The buildings weren't exactly squared off thanks to the building planners who hadn't paid attention in tenth grade geometry, and the contractors getting paid by the hour instead of by the job. That left huge amounts of unused space and lots across Norfolk that rarely saw the light of day. These lots were great when you wanted a meeting that no one would interrupt, especially when you needed lots of room and not a lot of witnesses.

Every so often some enterprising entrepreneur would get the bright idea of putting something behind those stores, be it storage areas or parking lots. That lasted about as long as it took the local gangs or organized crime families to convince the businessman that those areas are just fine as they were. Some got the hint from a couple hundred grand in their bank accounts. The ones who didn't get it got it rather soon after people they cared about started to go missing, or legs started getting broken. It rarely went that far, but accidents of bravery were known to happen.

The backs of coffee shops, bookstores and other small businesses watched over impassively as I was directed to the middle of a clearing of buildings. All around me was brick and metal and mortar, and not a damned bit of help anywhere to be seen. There was some obvious work being done, since there was scaffolding everywhere. No workers, though I could see where they had been, and recently. The overall effect was like being in an empty Thunderdome, and all I needed was Tina Turner to start singing to set the mood.

I stopped walking when I was in the middle of the clearing. My four escorts seemed to move in unison, keeping me flanked and in sight at all times. At this point, I raised my hands, put them behind my head and said over my shoulder, "You mind telling me what this is about? I'm trying to work here."

"That would be the poor decision you made, Statford."

"Everyone's a critic," I sighed. "Have you been talking to my mother?"

For the first time, Gunguy seemed to be flummoxed. "What?"

"She never wanted me to be a PI," I explained, all the time gauging the distance between the four. My left wingman was edged a bit closer than my right, while the point man, even though farther ahead of me, was too far to help quickly if things went wrong. "I told her it was either this or a Chippendale dancer." Point man was dressed in street clothes, which could let him move more quickly; the wingmen were in what looked like very uncomfortable suits that wouldn't react well to stress. "She didn't like that answer."

"I do not like that answer." There was a twinge of amusement in the statement, with that voice approximately eighteen inches away, four inches down.

"Like I said," I shrugged. "So who did I piss off this time?"

"You were the last person to see Jiao Shen-jing alive." Any warmth in the voice was gone. Down to business, then.

"So? She wanted to hire me for a job. What do you care?"

That earned me a jab in the back. He either had a hand cannon, which I doubted, or a suppressor, which was much more likely. Either way, it hurt. "What was the job?"

I sighed, rubbing my jabbed back with my left hand. "She wanted to know about a coin she had gotten in the mail. No big deal."

Another jab. "I think you're lying."

"Of course I'm lying. I always lie when I have a gun in my back, dick." That got me a vicious push with the gun. "I swear you will eat that godsdamned gun if you poke me again. I've got no quarrel with you all."

"Why did she come to you?"

Screw it. I wasn't getting paid for client confidentiality anymore. "She wanted to know who wanted her dead. Told me a tale about getting something in the mail that seemed to spook her, so she hired me to find out who sent it and why." I raised my left hand above my head again. "Apparently, the bad guy got to her first. Case mostly closed."

I heard some shuffling behind me, then some more Chinese, so fast I couldn't even begin to translate it even if I spoke the language. Gunman said something first, apparently to Pointman, then to the wingmen. "What else did she tell you?"

"Not a damned thing. I didn't get much of a chance to find out anything about her or whoever was hunting her before she died."

"I don't believe you." The words were flat, devoid of any emotion.

I dropped my hands; this was getting

ridiculous. "Fine, she told me something. Very important, since she was *fu shan chu* of your little club, wasn't she?" I referred to her being the deputy master of the Triad, since I doubted she had enough seniority to be the "mountain master", or *shan chu* of her particular group. Amazing what a few minutes of research can do for stacking the deck. That raised Point man's eyebrows. I had their attention, at least for the moment. "She said---" and I mumbled a bit.

"What did you say?"

"I said---" and I mumbled, even more incoherently this time. I could feel the distance closing between Gunman and myself.

"Speak up! I cannot understand you when you mumble!" One more vicious jab with the gun, right in the lowest lumbar vertebrae.

Some people just don't listen.

"I said, who run Bartertown?" Gunman drew back the gun to poke me again, but I wasn't there. At least, my back wasn't. I spun quickly to my left, nearly rolling over him vertically before ending up behind him. My right hand snaked around his, moving with all the speed I could muster. My left arm wrapped around his neck and squeezed, while the gun, a small .22 automatic pistol with a large suppressor on the barrel, was moved by me to aim at three targets. My finger had entered the trigger guard, and I pulled the trigger three times.

One red dot appeared on the right legs of each of the former gunman's compatriots, with screams and blood flowing from the wounds. A .22 would do very little damage in a gunfight, but you know when you've been shot with one. All three fell to the ground, clasping the knees and screaming for mercy, or deliverance, or whatever the hell it was they wanted. Their English ability seemed to had left them in a lurch. More was the pity.

I brought the gun to the man's head, the hammer back fully, a fresh bullet in the chamber. The suppressor did not completely erase the sound of gunfire, a Hollywoodism that never seemed to die, but persisted in spite of all the evidence otherwise. I could tell from the sounds made by the bullets firing that subsonic rounds were used, which would lower the overall noise. The suppressor ate a good portion of the rest of the noise, so the loudest thing seemed to be the action of the slide as it ejected the shell casings. It was a beautiful weapon, probably custom-built, and it was a damned shame this guy had his hands on it.

Formerly had his hands on it, as I felt him start to go slack from the chokehold. His hands clawed fruitlessly at my arm, trying to get even a small gulp of air. It was useless, and stopped when I smacked the business end of the pistol against his head. "Finally you get smart," I said. "I warned you, didn't I?" When I got no answer, I pushed him to the ground and gave the idiot orders to kneel in front of me, heels crossed, hands behind his head. The other three were still hollering from their wounds, so I said in my best bedside manner, "Shut up, you assholes, or I'll make sure you have something to cry about!" When that didn't work, I fired a shot at the point man, missing his head by about three inches. He shouted in surprise, then got quiet. The wingmen saw what I did and followed suit.

"Okay, my fun-meter has been pegged," I said. "Let's play a game. You tell me why you want to know so much about the case, I make sure the last thing you see isn't a bullet exiting your godsdamned skull." Another lack of response. "So that's how you want to play it?" Silence. "I promise you, this is not the time to screw with me or act like a tough guy. I have four of you, three with bullets lodged in your legs. I could shoot the wounded three and get what I need from you, my friend," I indicated the idiot, "by any means necessary. Or," I chuckled, "I could just kill all four of you and go about my merry way. I don't really care at this point. Convince me otherwise."

"We were just supposed to find out what happened to her, man," Pointman said through gritted teeth. His pants leg was dark purple from the mix of blood and jeans.

I smiled. Seems I can be a bit intimidating. "See? That wasn't so bad, was it?" Gunman didn't like that I was getting answers, but at that point, I really didn't give a sweet shit. "Next question: Who sent you after me?"

"Our *shan chu*. He wanted to know why she was dead and why you were looking into it!"

"So the first thing you do is try to abduct me? Kids these days," I said as I shook my head. With a kick to the former gunman's left foot, I told him to get up. "Call whoever you need to for these guys. Each of you owes me one. We clear?"

"The fuck you mean we owe you?" the right-side wingman shouted, blood still coming out from between his fingers. "You shot us!"

"And you're still alive to bitch about it." I let that sink in as I disassembled the pistol. As I thought, it was a work of art, and what I was about to do was almost criminal. The slide popped off in my hand, and I threw it into a nearby open dumpster. The spring got bent out of true and likewise tossed elsewhere. I slipped the suppressor into my pocket but flicked the barrel away. Finally, I popped each bullet out of the magazine one by one before sending the rest of the pistol to the four winds. "You'll thank me later." I turned to walk away, then heard the scuffing of a shoe. I stopped on a dime and said without turning around, "You didn't disarm me of my own gun, and I assure you, I won't shoot you in the leg. Don't even think it."

When I didn't hear anything more, I started walking again. I reached the street with no problems, then took a hard right to continue to the museum. If my luck held, I would be caught in a gang fight between the Furies and the Titans, with the Fae stopping by to kick me while I was down. After all, it's not like it hadn't happened before. Fortunately, my luck was better than usual and I made it the rest of the way to the museum without incident.

A quick check of the current guard's fingers confirmed that Luc's people preferred the later shift. I smiled tightly as I made my way through the exhibits again, though there were a lot more people this time. I took a different route, this time through a wing featuring mythology of different civilizations. Since it was a weekday, there were quite a few schoolkids walking around, and several teachers were running herd on the little rugrats. As I walked by, I heard some of the older children discussing an exhibit, a diorama of Baba Yaga, the epitome of mythical Russian witches, in all her dubious glory. Baba Yaga's hut towered over the kids by several feet, the chicken legs sticking out of the bottom of her home in excruciating detail. The hut itself was pretty large, and it looked rather detailed and well-made, with the wood looking worn, the little trinkets and bones on strings clicking and clinking in the slight breeze. I could see a glow coming from inside the hut, low and green and slowly pulsating.

Baba Yaga herself looked, well, terrible. She was everything a witch should look like, and she was fearsome. Her skin was dry leather, wind-worn and wrinkled, and her hair was white straw, like bleached hay. The fingers were claws, arms were sticks covered in rags, a hooked and sharp nose that smelled for Russian men, scraggly teeth exposed in a smile. Baba Yaga's eyes, though, were what caught me. They had the same pulsating glow as the hut, and pulsed in time with each other.

Shit.

"Come on, you pussy, touch it," one of these fine young idiots said. "It's not real."

The three kids were probably in their pre-teens, which went along with their IQs. All three were boys, and wore whatever clothes were in style these days. Two had their hats on backwards, and one of them had his pants hanging off his ass. The third, the one being called a pussy, wore the same clothes uncomfortably, like he had no desire for the world to know what color his underwear was.

"Yeah, man, it's just some stupid statue. What are you afraid of?" the other idiot said.

The third kid, who was probably smarter than the other two combined, shrugged like one of those emo kids I keep seeing on television. He muttered something and reached out his hand toward the exhibit.

Double-shit.

"That's enough, boys, off you go," I said just before contact was made. I could hear a frustrated growl in my head, but I ignored it. "Bad things happen to young people who touch things they shouldn't."

The first kid, who apparently had been given only the very best in the teaching of manners, said, "Who the fuck are you?"

"Museum security, and your ass couldn't cover what it would cost to fix this setup."

"Shit, how would you know, asshole?" Such a lovely child.

"Because your pants are just about on the ground, kid." I beckoned over one of the older ladies standing nearby. "Ma'am, are these yours?"

She was a pretty little lady, younger than me, with an easy smile that screamed "new teacher" on her face. "No, but I can find out. Thank you, sir." She led the Three Amigos away, admonishing them with whispered words while I got closer to the exhibit.

"Don't even think about it," I muttered. "Any of

these kids go missing, I know who's responsible, and it won't go well for you. Dig?"

Oh, you're no fun anymore, came the voice in my head. It was a syrupy-sweet sound, like honey and sugar and molasses, and it dripped slowly into my mind. It wasn't a pleasant feeling, like bathing in syrup from a soda fountain. *Can't a girl enjoy herself a bit?*

I put steel in my voice and my mind. "Not in my town. Your idea of fun is too messy. Have a nice day. Try the Jersey Shore. You'd fit in perfectly."

There was a cackle and she was gone, both from my mind and from the exhibit, which didn't look as fearsome as it did. It's never easy riding herd on gods and demigods. For them, "fun" is taking a young boy on a trip across multiple dimensions and maybe leaving a piece of him in each as a souvenir. The cleanup for something like that is rather messy, and I didn't want to add something else to my already full plate.

I made my way past all the kids, and back into the administrative area of the museum. The noise level was a lot less, and I could hear muted conversations all around me from behind closed doors. It wasn't that the speakers were loud, but because it was so quiet. The hall itself was dimly lit, almost like entering a cave or a mausoleum. My shoes made light squeaking noises on the tile. First a left, then a right turn, then back to where the professor used to have his office. Even though it had been a recent departure, I imagined they had found at least a temporary replacement for the job of curator.

When I reached the professor's old office, I saw that the door was open. Normally, I wouldn't have been worried, until I heard the sound of something dropping, and a muttered curse in a foreign language. Another bump, another curse. It was a language I was becoming intimately familiar with.

Chinese.

Dammit.

Putting my right hand under my coat, I gripped my Beretta and thumbed off the safety. From what I could hear, there was only one person in there, but I had been wrong before. The hallway terminated in this office, so I had no worries about whoever it was getting away other than getting past me. I could see light coming from the office through the glass on the door, but it was muted light, probably from a desk lamp. Whoever was in there was trying to be unnoticed, but also able to see. From my memory, I knew there was a heavy desk in the office, with filing cabinets lining the walls. The professor likely hadn't taken much with him, so the big furniture was probably still there. I created a map in my mind of where anyone would and could take cover if, for example, I busted in there and someone pulled out a machine gun to try and perforate me. These things happen.

I kept my body to the right of the door, where the hinges were and no one could see a silhouette framed perfectly for target practice. With my left hand, I pushed the door farther open. There was no sound from the hinges, and no sound from my gun coming out of the shoulder holster. I let the door open slowly until it stopped gently on its own. Edging closer, I looked past the threshold and saw someone in an over-sized coat with their back to me, leaned over the desk near the back of the office. Whoever it was wasn't tall, but the coat and the darkness may have fooled me. The distance from whoever it was to me was about fifteen feet, and I had them dead bang. It was just a question as to how I wanted to play this. The best idea would be to play it cautious. After all, I had no clue whether I was dealing with a lone robber, or a psycho killer, or the way my day had been going, both.

So of course, I played it like a smartass.

"The professor usually kept a bottle of Jack on the left side of the desk," I said, loudly enough to make sure I was heard. "And he never kept anything valuable in that thing; all the other drawers stick too easily." When the figure started to turn at the sound of my voice, I clicked my tongue against the roof of my mouth. "I really wouldn't do that. I don't miss thieves, especially from this close. You mind getting your hands where I can see them? I'll feel a lot better, especially since I won't have to shoot you. I've kind of hit my quota of letting people go for the day."

Hands were raised, and at my command, raised higher above the head. The hands were thin and covered in leather gloves. At another command, the hands went behind the head, fingers clasped. Lastly, I had the thief get down on his knees and cross his ankles. I took a glance behind me to make sure I wasn't going to get a surprise like I did outside. With the hallway empty, I moved a bit closer to my prisoner, the barrel of my pistol locked on the back of his head. "This just isn't your lucky day, is it?" I mused. "Wanna tell me why I shouldn't call the cops for trying to break into a curator's office?"

My cocky attitude was met with an unnerving silence. I had had enough of the silent tough guys as I could take anymore. After awhile, it just got boring. And aggravating, not to put to fine a point on it. I had learned from the other side of the barrel that aggravating someone with a weapon was a bad idea. As I made my way around to the thief's right, something familiar about the figure niggled at my mind. "You aren't that smart, either," I continued. "Always have a lookout if you're stealing. Now, on your feet."

The figure stood and my jaw hit the floor. Blood roared in my ears as I saw the face of one I had last seen staring sightlessly into oblivion. The lips, though unpainted, were the same, the skin tone was the same, the shape of the eyes was the same. It was Jiao's face, which meant...

"Deng Shin-jeng, I presume?"

Her right eyebrow raised in amusement, she responsed, "Since you know who I am, I take it I can put my hands down?"

I nodded, saying, "I was actually looking for you. You're in great danger."

"I usually think I am when someone is pointing a gun at me." Seeing that, I put the gun back into my coat with a sheepish look. "Now, would you mind telling me who the hell you are and why you felt the need to try and execute me in my own office?"

The steel that seemed to be genetic to her family shone through, and I was rather pleased there was some of it showing in the twin. It would make explaining things so much easier. "Miss Shin-jeng," I began.

"Please call me Dee," she interrupted. "No offense, but you sound like the most Chinese you use is when you order General Tso's chicken." Her accent was a mishmash of north London with an unmistakeable dash of New York. Trust me, it works. "As for telling me I'm in great danger, the only one threatening me is you with a gun to my back."

I really seem to have a way with women, don't I? "Sorry, ma'am. I had a nice little run-in with some street punks on my way here, and I was a little antsy."

Dee leaned against her desk and crossed her arms over her coat, giving me a skeptical glare. "How many?"

"Four," I shrugged.

"And not a mark on you?" The skepticism became outright disbelief. "If I believed it, I'd be impressed."

I rolled my eyes. Though it was said playfully, I was starting to get bored with this better-than-thee bullshit. "Anyway, I've got to get you out of here before something bad happens."

"Like what? Some idiot with a gun coming to abduct me? I think the worst has already come."

My voice became a whipcrack, no louder than conversation, but harder than steel. "No, lady, the worst will be some huge fire god come to crush your heart in your godsdamned chest, just like he did to your sister."

Dee went pale. "My sister's dead?"

Oh, shit.

Like a light switch, the superiority drained from Dee's face. It was eerie, as I had seen a lighter version of it just the day before from my first client, but it was similar enough to make me shudder. Tears began streaming from her eyes, down clean cheeks, dripping to her coat and the floor. She seemed to rock back from my words, and it occurred to me just slightly too late that she probably didn't know about her sister's untimely demise. She lurched and leaned forward, starting to silently cry, her mouth open, sobs so huge they couldn't escape her throat.

Like I said, I have such a way with women.

I stood there, feeling like the world's grandest asshole, and waited for her to finish. It's not that I'm cruel; far from it. I felt that it would have been intrusive, especially considering how I had broken the news. I likely would have gotten socked in the mouth for trying to be kind after such harsh words, and I had had enough of being knocked unconscious by women the last few years. So I just stood in the doorway, waiting until she had calmed down enough for me to say anything that would be understood. I knew I had screwed up, though; this was definitely going to bite me in the ass at a most inopportune time.

Several minutes passed before the storm finally subsided. It was a gradual tapering off, and it still hurt my heart. "I'm sorry, ma'am," I said, trying to console as best I could without putting my foot in my mouth any farther than I already had. "I know this is a bad time, but I need to know: did you receive a gold I Ching coin? Maybe through the mail or something?"

The baleful, hate-filled stare she gave me hit me with a physical force, making me take a step back. Her eyes, puffy and red, looked more at home on a demon's face than a human's as she reached a claw of a hand toward me. "You fucking bastard! My sister's dead and you want to talk about fucking coins?"

I spoke quickly, hoping for once the words came out right. "Your sister got one a few days before she died, and it was found on her. I'm trying to find out who sent it to her."

"What does it matter?" Her other hand came up as she approached me, looking ready to throttle me.

"Because whoever sent it to her also sent her assassin," I said, "and if the pattern holds, you're next."

That seemed to get through to her. "She came to you."

I nodded. "She knew someone had sent her the coin, but she thought it was just a message at first."

"Wait, you mean something reached into her chest and actually crushed her heart?" Dee's eyes went wide. "That's not possible."

"It's very possible. Not sure why you haven't been contacted yet regarding her death, but at this point it's beside the point." I reached into my coat pocket and produced a clean handkerchief. She took it gently. "Ma'am... Dee, I can't help you unless you help me. Did you get a coin?"

She closed her eyes and nodded, putting the handkerchief to use. "That's what I was looking for when you came in," she said. "I had gotten it two days ago."

"Have you touched it?" I asked. "I mean, with your bare skin."

Dee looked at me incredulously, that former superiority showing through. "Of course not. I'm a trained archeologist. I'm not stupid enough to do---" and she stopped herself as she realized what her late sister had done. The tears welled up again, but she covered her eyes quickly and took several deep breaths. After a few moments, she looked at me. "So who are you?"

"Tom Statford. I'm a private detective. I knew the professor here before you."

"Yes, I think he mentioned you, but only in passing." That kind of stung. I thought I had made a bit more of an impression than that. "How do you know my sister?"

"She came to me for help." I shrugged a bit as I took a glance down the hall. Still dark, still empty. "Dee, we have to move."

"Once I find the coin. I need it."

"Don't worry. I've got one." I didn't think I needed to say where I got it.

Her face clouded over as she realized the source. "Yes, but mine has the actual packing slip. I can probably trace it with that." Smart girl. "There it is!" she shouted in triumph as she gripped up a piece of paper. "I need to get more organized if I'm going to run this place."

"I'll get you some nice binders later," I said. "Now, let's get out of here."

I led the way, keeping my right hand on my stomach, the better to reach my gun. I had been hoodwinked once; that wasn't going to happen again. As Dee kept pace with me, my eyes darted everywhere, looking for more conventional assassins. Someone had it in for this family, and might not be too particular if one member was on the straight and narrow.

When we reached the central lobby, I felt less exposed thanks to the dozens of people filtering past the exhibits. It looked like the field trip was over, as there were no more kids in sight. This was a museum, which made it a public place and relatively safe ground for people trying to hide in plain sight from killers, pissed-off ex-whatevers, and mythological creatures who want to wear your skin because it goes well with a pair of earrings.

Don't laugh. It happens more often than you think.

I was hustling Dee fast across the floor, not wanting to push my already-pushed luck. She was taking her time, patting herself down for one thing or another, muttering to herself. Inwardly, I smiled, as I could tell which twin had gotten all the coolness. That smile died rather quickly when I thought about what she had gone through to get that coolness. In fact, it was a coldness, one Jiao had learned the hard way.

She was the yin to Jiao's yang. Jiao and Deng were perfect opposites, but not opponents. Pretty much everyone thought that the symbol meant the two forces were enemies, when nothing could be further from the truth. They were simply complementary opposites, defining each other with what they were not. Neither force was good, and neither force was evil. Just opposite sides of the same coin.

I pushed through a group of people leaving one of the halls, automatically reaching back to grasp Dee's wrist. No reason to lose her in the press of the crowd. There seemed to be a hell of a lot of people moving through this one hallway, and I had to twist and turn and nearly dance through the crowd. Dee muttered something a bit louder and grabbed my own wrist with a panicky grip, pulling her coat closer around her. The leather was soft, but there was an iron fist in that glove.

We finally made it past the tide of humanity into an empty part of the museum, and I mean empty. I looked back the way we had come and realized that I had gotten us turned around and sent down a different way that put us farther into the museum instead of closer to the exit. I also realized that we were in trouble as the fire doors slammed shut, with two rather large mooks helping the metal doors shut. The cavernous room echoed from the doors, the sound bouncing from one empty wall to another. There were a couple of other booms, which were likely the other exits from this room. The marble floors were bare, with no carpets and no guideposts with the ropes between them. There were no exhibits in this room, but a couple of ceiling decorations depicting a red-faced warrior wearing a green robe had been left hanging. There were some high windows that let in some light from outside, and a few empty stands where treasures had once been displayed.

Oh, and an even dozen guys were encircling Our Hero and the damsel in distress, and there was murder in their eyes. "Thomas Statford?" one of them said.

"If I say yes, what do I win?" I was gauging distances and angles, trying to take into account all the variables.

"An ass-whipping. You've disappointed the general."

I narrowed my eyes. "Then my name is Throatwobbler Mangrove, but it's spelled Raymond Luxury-Yacht." Apparently they weren't Python fans.

"You were supposed to be looking for the general's granddaughter, not having a date with---" and his words cut off in surprise.

And as he looked beyond me to the damsel, the surprise turned into hatred. He spit something that had to be a curse in Chinese, as it was too full of fury to be anything else. My heart sank as he pulled out a pistol and shouted an order to the others with him.

I took a deep breath.

Closed my eyes and released Dee's wrist.

I let my breath out, opened my eyes--

Gripped my gun from beneath my coat…

And then things got loud.

Chapter Eight

There's art to a gunfight.

I know how that sounds, but it's true. Any idiot can spray bullets and hope they hit something; that's been proven often enough by the psychos who shoot up innocents in movie theaters and schools. Someone throws enough metal in the air, they're going to hit something just by the law of averages. Rather pathetic, if you ask me. Knowing where the bullets will go, where to stand, how to stand, the angles of attack, the lines of the weapon molded into the body and vice versa. It's poetry in destruction, mixed with a little salvation when it's your ass on the line. There's art and beauty to a real gunfight. There are also two very important rules.

Shoot first and don't miss.

The familiar weight of the Beretta filled my hand with comfort, and I brought the barrel up in line with my first target: the gun hand of the guy directly in front of me. A scant ten feet separated us as I fired the first bullet. I couldn't have missed if I tried. The bullet struck the revolver he had pulled out, sending it flying through the air with the greatest of ease. Like something out of a movie, he grabbed his hand and screamed in a mixture of pain and rage. I closed the distance and sent my foot straight up between his legs, my attack bending him over enough for me to deliver the coup de grace to the back of his head with the butt of my pistol.

I crouched and swiveled in time to miss several bullets whizzing by two feet above me. My pistol barked three times, rapidly, two rounds hitting guns and destroying the weapons, the third striking a target in the right elbow. There was a spray of blood from the joint, and a shrieking coming from the freshly wounded thug. I wanted to put a shot through his mouth to shut him up, but some cold part of my mind knew that the noise would help me with a little psychological warfare as I was still outnumbered eight to one.

By this time, about six seconds had passed, from the barked order to old Shrieky McWhinerson bleating on and on about a shattered joint. My eyes picked out a likely place to make a stand if needed, but the enemy still had too many guns and too many people. Likely the daytime guards had been co-opted or replaced by these goons, so I couldn't depend on cavalry on that front. I had an extra magazine for the Beretta and an archeologist worth very little in the current surroundings. The bad guys were armed with pistols of their own, which they wielded with the skill of drunken rednecks high on meth and moonshine. While normally that isn't something to worry about, as I said before, when enough metal is in the air, something's getting hit, and I didn't want it to be me or the archeologist I had brought into this.

Staying still would pretty much assure my getting a visit from the Grim Reaper, so I kept moving, diving forward and rolling. I pushed myself to my left and fired again, another trio of bullets finding their marks. There were more screams of pain as a hail of return fire gouged out marble from the floor where I had been crouching not a second prior. I smiled grimly as I whirled myself around, letting my coat slip off my left arm. Another clockwise turn and I transferred my pistol to my left hand so my coat could fly off my right side to give them something else to shoot at. I had them down to five, which had to give them a moment's pause. There was also one other thing in my favor.

I was completely silent as I fought, while they were screaming. Seeing seven of your comrades taken down in ten seconds by one guy, especially the first friend taken down with such brutality, can be a good argument for stopping and thinking you might be in over your head. It was also rather telling that they had yet to take any form of cover. That told me two things. One, they hadn't expected to get into a gunfight today. That little fact was probably the only thing that had saved me from having these idiots set up to cover me as I walked in. It probably was originally just going to be an attempted ass-whipping. While I'm not a fan of said occurrences, I likely could have talked my way out of it.

The second thing it told me was these guys weren't on the general's direct payroll. They were sloppy, uncoordinated and likely just below "henchmen" on the evil overlord list. There were about two dozen places to hide from a gunfighter, and they just stood their ground, blasting away, like they had no idea what the word "cover" meant, and every movie stereotype of better living through superior firepower had been ingrained upon their souls, and they would absolutely win because they have bigger guns.

Anyone will tell you: It's not the size that

counts. It's how you use it.

My eyes saw the remaining five had formed a ragged line, staggered a bit, but straight enough that I might as well have been at a firing range. Pistol, submachinegun, pistol, SMG, pistol. As my coat twisted away, I slid across the marble floor and snapped off two rounds at the two bad guys with the submachineguns. Their hands shattered, and they screamed, their fancy German guns ruined by the impact of my bullets. I had ended up behind a display, taking just long enough to check myself quickly for any damage. Finding none, I reloaded the Beretta and tossed the almost empty magazine to my right, a second before diving to my left.

The human eye is attracted to movement, but is slow to react to multiple stimuli. Part of that whole hunter/gatherer thing from when the peak of human vocabulary was "Ook!". When we hunt, we focus on the fast-moving objects, especially when they come from where we know our prey is hiding. Problem is, it's pretty easy to distract someone with the trick I had just done. Remember, folks, just because a trick is old doesn't mean it won't work.

I took the two outside guys out with two bullets, one to the gun, one to the shoulder. Neither one would work properly again until after extensive repairs, and I was perfectly okay with that. I rolled to a stop and came up with my gun barrel aimed right between the eyes of the lucky guy who had been left standing. He had stopped firing when I had disarmed his two friends, the slide on his pistol open on an empty chamber. We stood there a moment, then he ejected the magazine and tried to put a new one in. I was impressed; trying to reload a weapon when someone's got you dead to rights is gutsy.

Not too bright, but gutsy.

I fired twice, the bullets passing his ears and missing by about half an inch. Two small tufts of his scruffy coarse black hair wafted to the ground. He flinched but held onto his weapon, the magazine not slid into the butt of the gun quite yet. I smiled slightly as his eyes widened. I dropped my cloak of silence and said, "No, that was not an accident."

He dropped his gun, the magazine clattering away.

"Smart." I kept my gun out but down, keeping my senses sharp as I looked to Dee. She had taken cover behind a low dais, and I saw quite a few gouges from bullets there. "You okay over there?"

She stood up slowly, eyes wide from what looked to be shock. Dee was completely stunned by the carnage, or relative lack thereof, that had been wrought by me. I was even impressed a bit; I knew I was good, but I had gotten lucky, too. Any of these idiots had shown more tactical common sense and it would have been case closed. Dee slowly nodded her head, her eyes guarded. From what I could see, she hadn't been hit, which was a minor miracle in and of itself.

Meanwhile, all around us were men bleeding and moaning, with several of them likely needing reconstructive surgery on their hands. Those I'd actually hit in the shoulder or arm were sitting up, holding their wounds with near-catatonic looks on their faces and whimpering. The only one without a mark on him put his hands up and behind his head. The guy was definitely impressing me with his grasp of just how to make me happy in this situation.

"Smarter." I approached him as his nearby companions looked at me with a mix of fear and hatred. "You can make me happier by doing me a little favor."

"I ain't talkin!" he shouted, which made my pistol come up from my side to connect and invisible line from the gunsight to his forehead.

"Shhh..." I said. "I don't want you to talk. If I did, I could probably make you sing like a canary. I have no interest in what you have to say to me." I stopped about ten feet away from him, making sure I kept the two men to his right and left in sight. "I want you to deliver a message for me."

"What message?"

I smiled broadly. "You tell Chip I'm just about to get on the General's job. I had a few loose ends to tie up. You can also tell him that if he ever even thinks about sending you goons after me again, I'll report your failure to him." I lowered the hammer on the pistol and put it in the holster under my arm. "You got me?"

The guy nodded. Not that there was much else for him to do, unless he wanted to have a dumbass attack and try picking up his fallen weapon. I glanced at the pistol, a rather nice Glock, and looked at him, shaking my head slightly. He got the message.

"Come on, Dee," I said as I went to retrieve my coat and my ejected magazine. The bullets hadn't done much damage to the coat, thankfully, but I'd need a needle and thread to repair it anyway. "I'm sure these boys will have a time explaining their way out of this. We can leave out that way, right?" I pointed towards the fire exit.

"Yeah," she said, her voice quiet. "That's the best way out."

I took her by the hand and we made our way out into the cold. It was bitterly cold, or the museum had been like a sauna. Regardless, the sweat of the gun battle was chilling against my skin, and the wind blew through the alley at high speed, lowering the temperature even more. The stone and brick walls sapped any warmth from the air, making my teeth start to chatter. I hate Virginia weather.

I let Dee's hand go long enough to put my coat on, then took it again as we walked quickly out the back alley of the museum. The alarm hadn't gone off, which told me this door was where they had come in. What clinched it were the dozens of unfiltered cigarette butts littering the ground of the alley, along with some fast food containers and a plastic cup. This set off some alarm bells in my head. I was being followed, which did nothing for my peace of mind and even less for my paranoia.

"They were waiting for me," I said. "I guess I pissed him off."

"Who?" We were moving rather fast as we exited the alleyway and into a crowd of people heading down Waterside Drive. "That was your fault?" Dee lowered her voice. "Why didn't you kill them?"

"Why would I kill them?" I kept my own voice

down, putting my arm around her shoulder to make sure our conversation stayed private.

"They were trying to kill you." I could almost feel her glare of incredulity. "Isn't that reason enough?"

"Two reasons: one, dead bodies don't work too well when the cops are likely on their way. Two, this makes them a lot less likely to come after me again with big guns."

"Why?"

"Because they know I could have used a dozen bodybags as a message and didn't." I looked at her. "Thought science-types weren't the violent type."

She smiled ruefully. "I doubt 'science-types' have been in situations like that very often."

I laughed a bit. "Touché." We ran across the street to the parking garage, where I hoped my car hadn't had any tampering. It wouldn't have surprised me if it had, though I tended to doubt it. After all, they were there to deliver a message and a beating, not a killing. Chip would not have done very well with the General if his men had actually killed me.

By the time we had reached the Beauty, the adrenaline from the gunfight had worn off and my knees started to feel a bit weak. I hate that feeling, but biology is biology, and adrenaline is adrenaline, and when it leaves, it leaves you weak. Before I did anything, though, I did a complete sweep of my car, checking the underside of it to see if anything had been added. While I knew of about eight ways to wire a car to blow that were undetectable, the mooks who had been sent after me didn't seem to have that kind of knowledge. However, I hadn't gotten to a ripe near-middle-age by trusting just to luck.

Training by my mother had me make sure the car was safe before I unlocked my passenger door for Dee and made my way over to my side. I unlocked my own door and sat down in the driver's seat, closing the door and leaning back with my eyes closed. My breathing was loud in my head, which was just starting to ring with the gunshots and the ricochets. That I could hear anything after that much gunfire was amazing, but I knew I'd pay for it later.

That is, if I had a later. After all, I had just, in one day, angered members of two very large groups of people with assets that could make my life rather miserable. My people skills apparently need some work. I made a promise to start reading and living by the words of Miss Manners for at least ten minutes if I got out of this case alive.

"So why come and save me?" Dee said, and I noticed she had a lot of her late sister's features. Yeah, I know twins are like that, but until you're face to face to face with a pair, it kind of blows your wheels. "Not that I don't appreciate the rescue, and I plan on rewarding you properly later, but you can't have known I was there."

I shrugged as I pulled my seatbelt on and started the Beauty. "I didn't know. I needed to know where these coins came from, and figured they had to be shipped from somewhere."

"Obviously."

"Yeah, and whoever sent them wanted to make sure the recipients got them. That means there's a paper trail. Not an easy one, but there is one. I find out who sent the coins, I can get this case over and done with and get on to another one that might be a little less hazardous."

"Like what? A dozen gun-toting thugs too much for you?"

"They were for the easier case," I chuckled. Driving the Beauty back to the interstate was deceptively easy. "The one I'm on now involves a torqued-off god of fire being used as an assassin, and I don't know why."

Dee scoffed at me. "You're serious? You actually believe in God?"

"Gods," I absent-mindedly corrected.

"Excuse me?"

"Gods, as in more than one." I sighed explosively. The adrenaline was fully worn off and I was getting snappish. "Look, here's the Reader's Digest version: all the gods that ever were exist. I get to act as a go-between with deities and mortals. Right now, someone decided to unleash a very powerful fire god who gets along with nobody onto six very unlucky people. Whoever gets one of those coins is not long for the world, courtesy of Chu-Jung."

"But why me?"

"Had something to do with your sister, I think." I tried to soften the blow. "She was into some not very nice things, in case you didn't know."

"My sister brought me over here from rural China," Dee said, and her voice dropped about a hundred degrees. "She put me through school, helped me get my green card, gave me everything.

Don't you tell me she's not 'nice'," she said, her voice twisting with derision.

"She was suspected of a lot of very bad things, up to and including murder, prostitution, human trafficking, and any number of other felonies and crimes against humanity," I shot back, jerking the wheel a bit to dodge cars and get in the fast lane.

"If she did what you said, why did she help me? That makes no sense."

I shrugged again. "Guilt? A desire to balance the scales? Who the hell knows? What does matter is your sister and four other people are dead by the same means, and all five of them got a gold I Ching coin, like the one you got." I sped past another idiot driving only five miles over the speed limit. "Now, I'm not the sharpest knife in the drawer, but that sounds like a pattern, and if I had one of those things and wasn't dead, I'd sure as hell be worried."

"But I haven't done anything!" Dee shouted, her voice cracking. "I've just lived the best life I know how!"

"Yeah, well, so did your sister." My voice cut off any further discussion on the point. "I don't know or care what you did, since I'm pretty sure you really didn't do anything. Do you know about the rest of your family?"

She got quiet at that. "I had... heard a few things, but my sister was always so good to me. She gave me anything and everything I needed, I didn't really think anything of it."

"Gifts designed to shut you up. Sounds about right." I shook my head. "Anyway, all five of the dead were very bad people. As far as where you fit in? Likely needs to be six targets to complete the set."

"Why?"

"The gods have rules, lady. They may not make sense to us mere mortals, but they have to follow them, whether they like it or not." I passed Willoughby Spit, which meant I wasn't more than fifteen minutes from the office, if I could get over the bridge first. "All that boils down to is I have to find whoever sent the coins and see if I can get you off the hook."

"While dodging demons and gods and thugs," she laughed. "Sounds impossible."

"I call that Thursday."

Dee roared with laughter. "A tough guy, I see."

"Just don't like innocent people getting hurt."

"Where are we going?"

"My office. I can get you there and safe for a bit, then I can see about getting a line on those coins through the shipping manifest."

"You mean the one I have?"

I shook my head. "The one I have, that I took from you while making sure you weren't hurt."

Dee slapped at her pockets and felt around in them, finding I had gotten away with my sleight of hand. "You son of a bitch."

"You'll get over it. Besides, I figured you'd use it as a bargaining chip to try and get involved." Before she could respond, I cut her off. "How about no? I have enough on my hands trying to keep you alive without you throwing yourself into this mess and getting yourself killed."

"You'll never find who sent those without me."

"I'll take my chances. I know a few people." Besides, I needed a day to work on my other case. Yeah, the general likely wasn't behind that attempted beating, but I didn't want to see one he was behind. One of those would likely involve high-powered rifles from very far away.

No need to tell Dee that, though.

We rode the rest of the way in silence, her fuming and me wondering just what a fire god could do if denied his prize. The Chinese pantheon didn't seem to be too particular about collateral damage, so it likely wouldn't be pretty. However, it's not like there were any real worries when it came to fire; the area was surrounded by water, and a fire would only go so far. Not exactly a comforting thought, but at least there was something that wasn't the end of civilization as I knew it on the horizon. Dark cloud, silver lining and all that.

As we drove over the bridge, I saw one of the two locally-stationed aircraft carriers moving over the water nearby.

Clarification: One of the *nuclear-powered* aircraft carriers.

Oh hell.

Once we got to my office, I directed Dee to have a seat while I did some searching. She still wasn't speaking to me, and I was okay with that; I wasn't really in the mood to play nice anymore. Things were starting to not make as much sense as they should, and I didn't have time to babysit someone who apparently had nothing to do with whatever had set this nasty bit of revenge into motion. That's what this was, though: revenge. Getting a god to do your dirty work isn't something someone does on a whim. These coins were designed for one thing, and that was to utterly erase six people from existence for some crime they had perpetrated.

The questions of who and why were still unanswered, and I had no clues, other than a dead crimelord and a shipping manifest from said crimelord's sister. I could discount Dee being involved in the why, since I doubted being an archeologist would cause someone to have that much hate. She seemed about as troublesome as dry paint, and from what Mac had given me about her, she was pretty much a zero when it came down to "reasons for someone wanting her dead".

That left Jiao and her dysfunctional family. I sat down behind my desk as Dee sat on the couch. I tuned her out as my mind took things a step further, calling back all the details I had read from the folders. It was a neat trick I had learned over the years, one that had served me well both personally and professionally. All five were highly placed in their organization, the equivalent of mob bosses except their word really was law, and with their deaths, there was now one hell of a power vacuum. That led to another train of thought: this might have been more than just revenge. It could be a power struggle that coincided nicely with good old-fashioned vengeance. In the criminal fraternity, one doesn't waste an opportunity.

Which led me to another thought. I pulled out

the thumb drive the General had given me. I had only gotten the thing a few hours ago, but I had put it off in a fit of pique. Break into my office, eh? I'll show you by not looking at your case! What are you going to do then, old man? Besides have your subordinate send a bunch of goons after me, I mean. Sometimes, I don't think my cunning plans all the way through. Looking at the two-inch-long piece of plastic, I figured I should at least see what was on it since it meant that much to him. I popped it into my laptop and started going through the files. It definitely made for interesting reading.

"What are you looking at?" Dee said, looking over my shoulder. I hadn't heard her come to stand behind me. That's what I get for thinking too hard.

"Just something regarding another case," I answered, my fingers tapping a few keys as I scrolled through a few documents. "No biggie."

"Another case? What about the one involving me?" She sounded worried. "Didn't you say some fire god is going to try and kill me?"

I tried to sound unconcerned. "I figure I have a few days before it comes to that, and besides, this might have something to do with your situation." I didn't hold out any real hope of that, but who knows? Stranger things have happened.

"You think so?"

"Maybe. It's worth a look, at any rate." I felt a twinge in my left shoulder, which I had landed on in the museum while ducking and dodging gunfire. My right hand moved to rub it to loosen it up.

Dee pushed my hand away. "Here, let me." Her fingers seemed to find the tense muscles in my shoulder and started to knead them. I felt them untie from the knots they were in instantly, and felt and heard a slight pop, usually a good sign. "Better?" I nodded, massaging the bridge of my nose. "Let me get the other side," she said, and I felt her begin to work on my right shoulder. I have to admit, it felt really nice.

"Didn't know archeologists had such supple fingers," I laughed, my eyes closed, my head leaning forward.

"You have no idea," Dee chuckled. "I have a great many talents."

"I'm sure you do," I said. "That really feels good." I felt my cares start to melt away. I hadn't realized just how tense I was until Dee started her impromptu massage. You have no idea how tired you are when a simple shoulder rub almost makes you conk out right then and there. I was starting to feel things untie both in my shoulders and in my mind.

Dee gave a self-satisfied laugh. "I bet it does. I'm very good at whatever I do."

A new voice cut through the room like a blade. "Yeah, I'll bet you are," Susana said, her tone dangerously neutral, her words completely spelling out my doom in no uncertain terms. "You work by the hour or by the stroke?"

All things considered, at that point, I would have preferred going head to head with a fire god.

My head snapped up and I pushed Dee's hands away, pulling myself together and bringing my mind back to reality. "Susie!" I said, looking at her.

Susana's face was flushed with anger, her eyes

narrowed and her jaw clenched. She stood at the door, wearing a thick coat, blue jeans and a look of hatred that would have made a demon run away not so bravely. "Oh, you remember me?" The flatness of her voice belied just how pissed she was at me, and I knew I was probably going to be in more trouble than I could possibly imagine. "I'm flattered. Didn't think you could remember anything with that---" Susana's eyes widened as she saw who was doing the rubbing. "What the hell are you doing here? Alive?"

I stood up abruptly to try and say something very intelligent under other circumstances. "Dee, would you mind waiting in the other room, please?"

The temperature dropped even further in Susana's voice, burning my ears. "You mean your bedroom?"

Like I said, under other circumstances. "Better idea! Susana, would you mind joining me in the other room so I can explain exactly everything that's going on?"

My hopefully not-soon-to-be-ex-girlfriend gave me a baleful glare before stalking into my bedroom. Dee was about to say something, but I held up a warning finger; the only voice Susana needed to hear right then was mine. Otherwise, it would likely… it wouldn't end well for me. In fact, it would probably get very interesting. How would I define "interesting"?

In the words of Hoban Washburn: "Oh god, oh god, we're all going to die."

As I closed the door behind me, I knew that I

would have to be very careful with what I said in the next few moments. I turned to face Susana and held my hands up in surrender. "I swear it's not what it looks like."

Susana's nose wrinkled as she crossed her arms in front of her. This was not a good sign. "Oh?" In one sound, she compressed every bit of scorn and derision a woman could muster. I can guarantee you, it's quite a bit. "It looked like another woman who looks like a dead hooker was giving you a shoulder rub."

I cleared my throat. "Okay, so it is what it looks like."

"And it looks like you were enjoying it."

"I wasn't trying to enjoy it. I was sitting there looking over some files and---"

"And the *puta* decided she was going to give the big strong man a massage, since it apparently runs in the family." Oh hell, she was breaking out the Spanish cuss words. "You've got fifteen seconds to explain who the hell she is before I dropkick your *pinche* ass from here to the beach and back."

I took a deep breath, hoping it wasn't my last, and started talking as quickly as I could. "She's the sister of the woman you saw yesterday and is an archeologist at the museum who doesn't have anything to do with the tongs and Mac checked her out and said she's clean and---"

Susana reached out with her hand and covered my mouth. "Her sister?" I nodded. "She has a twin sister?" I nodded again. "What kind of bullshit is that?"

I said something, but was muffled by her hand.

She removed her fingers from my lips. "The kind of bullshit that I seem to have to deal with on too regular a basis."

"An archeologist?" Susana shook her head in disbelief. "*Dios mio*, you come up with some crazy shit, Tommy." She sat on the bed and crossed her legs. "So what's she doing here?" I was about to talk and she injected, "Besides making me want to beat her ass?"

"She's Jiao's twin sister," I began, leaning against my dresser. "Totally legit, from what Mac found out. She got one of the coins, but it doesn't look like she's in any danger from the coins, at least so far as I can tell." I rubbed my face with my hands, trying to put things back together. "Problem is, it looks like the tongs are looking for whoever killed Jiao, and might get the dumb idea of using Dee in there as bait."

My girl raised her eyebrow. "Dee?"

"She said I can't pronounce her name right." When Susana made no further verbal comment but narrowed her eyes at me even more, I continued. "Anyway, someone came after me at the museum when I went to talk to the professor."

"Olafssen? How's he doing?"

"Retired, thanks to a lottery win." I nodded my head to the door. "Guess who got appointed his replacement. You might hear rumblings from the Norfolk cops about a fracas that happened in one of the empty parts of the museum."

Susana exhaled heavily. "That's one of the things I was coming over to talk to you about. They said there was some kind of gunfight over there."

I made a disgusted noise. "Pure self-defense, and no one was killed."

"Yeah, well, they're still looking into it. So why bring her here?"

"I think someone's using the coins to not only even a score, but to make a move on the local Triad organization," I said. "Jiao was a big mover in the area, and the other four who got killed were big shots, too."

"You think someone's trying to take out the competition?" Susana shook her head. "Isn't using whatever the hell they're using like using a nuke to kill a cockroach? There have to be easier ways to get revenge."

I laughed lightly and without humor. "Not if you also wanted to send a message while you're taking power."

Susana stood and looked at me. "What kind of message?"

"The kind that makes you think twice about fucking with the one sending it." I rubbed my chin. "Of course, the big drawback is this kind of message has a way of backfiring, and backfiring in a big way."

"How big?"

"Nagasaki sounds about right." She winced. "That's why Dee's here: So I can focus on who sent the damned coins to begin with."

"You want me to keep an eye on her?"

This time I raised my own eyebrow. "You promise not to kill her?"

"She keeps her hands to herself, yes."

"Okay, then, you got it. Just keep her here

while I make a run."

"Where do you think you're going?"

I remembered some of the things I read from the files the general had given me. Damned if I shouldn't have known where I'd end up. "Chinatown."

Susana whistled low. "Pack an extra gun, *gringo*. I want to make sure you come back."

My hand was rested on the doorknob, my eyes closed. "Believe me, I have no desire to go there, but I think that's where I'll find a few answers. Let's hope I have the right questions."

We exited my bedroom, me first, then Susana. Dee was sitting on the couch, smiling plainly. She had taken her coat and gloves off, and was reading through a copy of People magazine Susana had left a few days prior. Even though I knew she was a twin, the resemblance was uncanny, and it seemed that I was looking at a Jiao that could have been, if only she had gone a different path. "For want of a nail," if I wanted to get poetic about it. I tried a smile on my face which felt only half-phony, and said, "Dee, this is Susana."

Dee smiled and said, "Your girlfriend, I take it?" I nodded. "Charmed, I'm sure, and such a charming lady she is."

I didn't have to look at Susana to know that Susana was about to rip her heart out. "Detective Marquez is going to keep you company while I make a quick run."

"She's a cop?"

"Yes, I am," Susana piped up, stepping in front of me, "and I'm standing right here."

"Detective Marquez is going to make sure nothing happens to you while I'm gone, Dee." I checked my phone for the time. Just after three in the afternoon. Time was flying, and I had no idea where it was going. "You can trust her like you trust me."

"I don't trust you," Dee said. "No offense, but you did sneak up on me with your gun out. Not a good way to earn brownie points."

"Fine, then," Susana said with a saccharine sweetness. "You can trust me like you should trust him. Tommy is probably the only person keeping you alive right now."

I caught the not-so-subtle implication and cleared my throat. "On that note, let me get out of here." To Susana, I said, "I'll let you know what's going on if I find anything." To Dee, I said, "Don't give her any trouble, please. She's one of the best people to have on your side in a scrap."

Dee snorted. "I'll believe it when I see it. Go on and do whatever you're going to do," she said, flapping her left hand at me. "The babysitter is appreciated, but not needed."

Susana's smile lost none of it's shine, and gained no sincerity. "Oh, I'm sure we'll be just fine, Tommy. You go on; I'll handle this." When I started to say something, she said through clenched teeth, "Go. Now."

And out the door I went.

Chapter Nine

Being a private detective isn't always gunfighting and fistfighting and fighting with your significant other over potential and actual misunderstandings. It can have its exciting moments, too, where you walk into someplace exotic and give a witty one-liner that freezes the bad guys in their tracks with the knowledge that you're there to chew ass and kick bubblegum. There are times where the detective, sure of what he's going to find, gets the villain, grabs the dame around the waist and kisses her as the credits roll.

And then, of course, there's my life, where the villain kicks the crap out of me, and I never think of good one-liners as I walk into a place. Also, I have to tell you, there is nothing at all exotic about the Chinatown of Hampton Roads. It's dull, it's commonplace, it's completely unremarkable.

Which is exactly how the citizens like it.

No one would know it, but there was a sizable Chinese population on the Southside, and it had been steadily growing larger over the years. Not all at once, of course, but at a controlled rate. If you knew where to look, you could find pockets of ethnic Chinese, and for the most part, they were law-abiding citizens of the area. Most of them were even natural-born citizens, second- and sometimes third-generation Americans. They had jobs, and families, and homes, and lives, just like everyone else. The American Dream, just like it says on the Statue of Liberty: "Give me your tired, your poor," and whatnot. Good people who just wanted a chance to make it in the land of opportunity.

There were, however, a few families who had brought with them more than just a desire to make it. These people had brought some unsavory business from their homeland, making sure that not just their people had an opportunity to flourish, but their vices had an opportunity to flourish as well. Those families brought their patience, and had begun decades ago, before World War Two, to set up their own enclaves, using signs none of the uninitiated could see, making a hidden city beneath a city. The tongs were a lot like the Mafia used to be, in a way: protecting their people from the predators who would attack the vulnerable. Of course, this protection came at a price, and the Chinese had had centuries to refine their various methods of vice and collection.

Norfolk had been chosen as the hub of the Hidden China, and it made sense for it to be a center point for any dealings, legitimate and criminal. There were the ports for incoming and outgoing goods, military bases and ships, and best of all, lots and lots of room for expansion and making things vanish. What made it even more perfect was no one would believe there was a kind of city-beneath-the-city, especially a Chinatown. Sure, people said, there were a few more laundries and restaurants, but that's just because "those people" were so industrious and hard-working. There's no Chinatown, they'd continue, because there weren't a bunch of streets with pagodas, paper lanterns and dragon statues. How could there be a Chinatown without dragon statues?

The answer was simple: the tongs weren't ready to make their presence known until they were sure there was nothing to stop them, legally or otherwise.

The area those in the know called Chinatown covered five pockets of Norfolk, each about five square miles. They were separated by "normal" streets and neighborhoods, and the borders were obvious to anyone who spent a few minutes watching people go from one area to another. The tongs always wore some kind of colored cloth, usually in the form of a bandana or sash, and they would always put it on as soon as they entered their turf. Not everyone Chinese was a part of the tongs, but everyone who was part of the tongs was Chinese.

Officially, the cops dismissed the idea of such a thing as Chinatown existing without them knowing about it. Cub reporters were laughed at by police spokespeople for bringing up the mythical Hidden City, and those reporters eventually learned not to bring such idiotic ideas up on the record. Unofficially, every police chief on the Southside was working with the Attorney General to find some way, any way, of slowing down the eventual rise of Chinatown, and all the illicit things that came with it. The odds were very long on their success, and in the meantime, Chinatown quietly grew and prospered.

Regardless of what I thought of the whole arrangement, I knew I needed some information, and I would only get it by venturing into the Hidden City. It was a risk, but I had a job to do, and if finding some guy's granddaughter helped me find who was targeting the heads of one of the local Chinese crime families, then it would hopefully be worth it.

Besides, I hadn't tempted fate and death in a couple of hours, and I was getting bored.

As I drove through a "normal" neighborhood, I kept my eyes open for the border signs. They are always small and unobtrusive, and I'd be damned if I would get caught entering Chinatown unaware. I wasn't too popular in a couple of the pockets, so I made sure I went to a pocket I wouldn't get shot the moment I drove in. I may have moments of bravery, but that doesn't mean I have to be stupid and leave myself open to attack. Getting attacked once in a day was not a big deal. Twice in a day was pushing it. Three times? My fun-meter was officially pegged, and I was starting to get the sense that either someone was screwing with me trying to get me killed, or just flat out trying to kill me. Whichever way it was, I didn't care. If the general had something to do with these coins, and at the rate things were going he likely was, I would find out one way or the other.

Another thing bugged me. Usually I didn't run into the Big Bad until they were trying to kill me, and even then they were kind of upfront about it, leaving ambiguity by the wayside. If General Wu wanted me dead, he could have done it that morning while I was out cold. There was also no reason to want me dead, besides having me out of the way for some ridiculous scheme or plot, and the general didn't seem like the kind of guy to risk everything just to put one in the brainpan of a private detective.

He was old, he was methodical and I got the sense he wanted me to find his granddaughter, for whatever reason. That meant he wanted me alive.

The files from the thumb drive had mentioned the *Jin hudie*, or Golden Butterfly tong, which was a Chinese street gang I knew quite well. They had also mentioned that the tong was not to blame for the disappearance. An odd statement, but considering the files were about as circuitous as a Mobius strip, I decided to just be thankful that I wouldn't be facing off against one of the "social clubs" of the Hidden City. These last few days had been nothing but odd statements and odd happenings, and coming from me, that was saying something.

I was so deep in thought, I missed the small flag depicting a golden butterfly, the outlying sign that I had entered tong territory. The roads were empty, which didn't help my catching obvious signs, and I didn't see one of the local watchmen raise his hand to me. That was soon remedied at the first stoplight in the worst way possible.

Like an idiot, I hadn't locked my door, and had forgotten I hadn't locked it, so when it flew open, I must have looked even dumber than I felt. A fist rocketed into my jaw, making my feet come off the pedals. The Beauty jerked to a stall and I felt like I was in a cartoon as I heard tweeting birds and saw stars. I hadn't been hit that hard in months, and I didn't relish getting hit again. The problem was, that punch must have been a reset button, as my limbs decided to mutiny and not answer my commands.

And things got worse. Oh so very worse.

My attacker unbuckled my seatbelt with about as much gentleness as a rabid wolverine before pulling me out of my car. I flailed my arms a bit before I smacked onto the road. I spent about a fraction of a second face planted before I felt the sharp pain of a boot into my side, lifting me up a few inches and making me bark out a cry of pain. I rolled onto my side and tucked into a ball, trying to protect my head. That earned me another vicious kick, this time to my spine. It stunned me further, making me straighten and knocking the wind from me. I tried to get my bearings and felt hands on my shoulders. My hands flew up to knock away my attacker, or at least I tried, but the most I managed was a fluttering. I was thrown into the side of my car, the back of my head hitting the metal of my car. My ears rang and I felt blood start to leak from a newly-opened wound.

"You ain't supposed to just drive through, *guilao*!" he said, throwing me against my car again. The voice sounded familiar, but I was too dazed to notice. "You know the rules!"

As I was held against the side of the Beauty with a forearm at my throat, I finally focused on who was beating the hell out of me. At apparently the same time, my attacker got a good look at me. I blinked hard and croaked, "Oh, hey Jimmy."

"Tommy?" It was almost comical, the way he blinked at me. "What the hell you doin here?"

I have such a way with people. I chuckled a bit just before I passed out.

Jimmy Chu had been born Frederick Wong, a

second-generation member of the Golden Butterfly
tong. He was an average Chinese guy, a bit taller
and huskier than from the old country thanks to the
hormones and crap that goes into our food. Jimmy
was also an enforcer for the Golden Butterfly tong,
and got his name from the fact he was both a
kickboxer and wore steel-toed combat boots
wherever he went. I had run into him a few years
ago on a case involving some Thai smugglers, and
we had worked together pretty well. After
extracting a promise from me that I'd let him handle
the "punishment" of the smugglers in exchange for
a bit of consideration when coming to his part of the
Hidden City, we parted ways amicably. It didn't
make me part of the Golden Butterfly tong, but it
meant I had standing enough not to be dismissed
out of hand. It also got me somewhat of an inroad
into the Hidden City, which was not anything to
sneeze at.

Of course, it also meant that if I followed the
rules, I wouldn't have bruised ribs, a sore spine and
a probable concussion to go along with my head
wound if I showed up unannounced in Golden
Butterfly territory. So I hadn't followed the rules, so
I paid the price.

Jimmy was falling over himself apologizing,
which consisted of my sitting in his kitchen at his
small house not too far from where I had gotten my
inevitable ass-kicking, his girlfriend shoving a tree
branch into the gash in the back of my head and
shouting at two of their kids to stop beating each
other up. Intellectually, I knew she was gently
dabbing a wet towel soaked in peroxide at the

wound, but if you've never had a head wound, trust me: she might as well have been using a jackhammer. Her name was Kuan Li, a sweetheart who had calmed Jimmy down over the last few years, giving him three kids and a reason not to be out running the streets with a private detective who had a pretty good reputation for being a badass.

Of course, she was seeing just how much of that reputation was deserved as I hissed at the pain from the chasm Jimmy had opened up.

"Oh, you a big baby!" she shouted, which was her normal tone of voice. Raising three kids who were each a year apart with English being a second language helped explain that. "I barely touch you!"

"Your boyfriend touched me enough, Kuan Li," I laughed, smiling so Jimmy wouldn't take offense. He looked sheepish but knew I had no hard feelings; I had broken the rules so I had paid the price. "I forgot how hard you could hit, Jimmy."

Jimmy smiled back, more at ease now that he wasn't doing a high-step into my ribcage. "I forget how good you take a beating, Tommy. What you doing around here?"

I reached into my coat and pulled out my phone, seeing there were a couple of calls from Harley's work number at the morgue. I had more important things to deal with, so I ignored it. I was checking the spelling of the missing girl's name, and the characters on the shipping label, which were in Chinese. "I need some help finding a girl and reading a shipping label."

Kuan Li poked me in the back of the head, making me gasp. "You already have nice girl! She cop!"

"Not that kind girl!" Jimmy shouted. "He not stupid enough to make her mad!"

"You think this is bad?" I shook my head gently. "She got through with me, they'd need a hose and a shovel to clean up the mess. Besides, I love her."

Jimmy's girl was more gentle with her next touch. "She nice girl!"

"I know. So you know where I can find information about Xu Bai Rong?"

Both Kuan Li and Jimmy went rigid, with him exchanging a look over my head to his woman, and I got the feeling I was about to get a pair of lies. "Never heard of her, *guilao*. Not anyone around these parts."

"Uh-huh." That was lie number one, but I was willing to let it slide for the moment. "How about you, Kuan Li? That name ring any bells?" I tried to turn to look back at her, but her hands were on the sides of my head, holding it steady. She couldn't lie to my face, so she did the next best thing.

"You two stop hitting each other or I come after you both!" she screamed at her kids. Kuan Li wasn't mad at them; they just made a convenient way to keep from answering my question. Suddenly she threw the towel onto my shoulder and said something in rapid Chinese at the kids. She pushed my head forward and ran after the two children, who giggled at their mother chasing them.

I picked up the towel and held it against the back of my head, wincing a bit, but knowing I had gotten the second of the lies. Taking a deep breath, I squeezed my eyes shut and focused on putting away the pain until later. The throbbing from the base of my skull lessened after a moment or two, but I kept the towel where it was, knowing that as soon as I pulled it away the blood would start to flow again. I opened my eyes to look at Jimmy, who looked abashed and ashamed, as well he should.

"Jimmy, who the hell is she." I wasn't asking anymore.

"She was bad news a couple years ago," Jimmy said haltingly. "She come from Old Country."

"You're acting like she's your Mountain Master," I said.

Jimmy shook his head at my mention of the head of a Triad. "No, she not *shan chu*."

"I kind of figured that, Jimmy. I may be *lao wai*," I used the slang term for "Anglo foreigner" that he had called me with some affection, "but I'm not stupid. Who is she?"

"Tommy, you don't want go this way," Jimmy said. "I ask you forget finding this girl. This not go good for you."

"She's dead, isn't she?" I didn't have to see Jimmy nod. "Gods, Jimmy, if she's dead, who the hell cares? I'm trying to find out what happened to her for---"

"General Wu Zhe Hou, yeah?"

Now it was my turn to be a little on the wary side. "Yeah. How'd you know?"

Disgust colored Jimmy's face. "I knew he try come find her, but of course he send someone else. Useless old man." Jimmy stood up and stomped from one side of the kitchen to the other. I could almost see the steam coming from his ears, and I could say I had honestly never seen him that pissed.

"Who was she to you, man?" I put the towel down on the table and kept my eyes on my host. Though Jimmy would honor the laws of hospitality, I could tell he was angry enough to possibly forget himself in the heat of the moment. He may only have been about five-foot-seven, but his temper was a lot shorter, and he hit like a fucking Mack truck.

"She was nobody to me, Tommy," Jimmy said, looking at the floor. "I not even know who she was until it was all done, and even then, there nothing I can do about it. You know I hate that, right?" He didn't see me nod, but I imagine he felt it. "She just some dumb girl got caught up in wrong thing, belong to wrong family."

"So what happened?" I had a really bad feeling where this was headed, but Jimmy needed to get it out in his way. Otherwise, he would close down and I'd lose my lead.

Jimmy looked at me. "I bring her where they tell me, she get picked up, I not see her again."

"Where'd you take her?"

"The Dragon Empress, man," Jimmy spat. "That bitch wanted her, so she got her."

Shit. Things just tied together in a really bad way. "Why'd she want her?"

"*Fukuan*." Jimmy said it like I understood Chinese.

"English, Jimmy."

"Payment, Tommy."

Holy shit. "She was sold?"

My host laughed for the first time in awhile.

"Hell no. It don't work like that. You not Chinese. You not know what my people like."

"Then make me understand, Jimmy, because what I'm hearing is some girl got sold like a piece of meat to somebody," I hissed, "and that's fucked up, no matter where you come from."

"Oh, you think it that simple, huh?" Jimmy stalked back across the kitchen, thrusting his hands in his pockets. I could see he had them knotted into fists, and I made an effort to dial back my own rage. "You think it just something someone order in catalog because she match the curtains?"

I sat forward in my chair, cradling my head in my hands. "Of course not, but what the hell did she do to deserve that?"

"Like I said, Tommy, she was payment. Someone owe a debt, they use her to repay it. She have no say in matter."

"Her grandfather?"

"I don't know who her *yeye* was, and I not care," Jimmy warned. "I already feel like shit over that girl, especially when I find out her *ba*, her dad, was the one who used her like that."

"Gods," I muttered. "What kind of father would do that to his own daughter?"

The answer came from the entrance to the kitchen. "The kind who in debt up to his eyeball with Dragon Empress." Kuan Li's voice was hushed for once, and I understood. She knew what being used as currency meant. Once upon a time, Kuan Li had been a working girl, and had done that kind of work for a couple of years. Kuan Li had been traded in that way, only it had been her mother who had sold her to a local pimp for six chases of the Dragon. After being broken in by her pimp, Kuan Li found her mother overdosed on three of the six doses of heroin. Jimmy had told me that she said she had left her mother where she lay, and to this day wouldn't speak of what happened between the time she had been selling herself and when Jimmy had swooped in like a damned superhero and saved her. "Her *ba* use her to pay debt to Dragon Empress, so she not have him torn apart like she did his wife."

I looked to Jimmy, my face betraying my disgust. "Torn apart?"

"It called 'Phoenix Suns Her Wings', and it as bad as you think."

"I don't want to know, do I?"

Kuan Li said, "It where someone hung by arms and legs from beam, and spin the beams." That she didn't flinch or seem squeamish at all told me she had seen such torture and worse. "She die eventually, and she die screaming."

"Girl's *ba* do it to save himself, yeah, but he save her, too," Jimmy shrugged. "Dragon Empress do that one herself, from what I hear." He looked at his girl, who nodded in confirmation. "That about three months before I get out of the bad stuff for good."

"What happened to her dad?"

Jimmy spit in disgust. "He fuck up good later on anyway, Dragon Empress perform the Five Penalties."

I winced. I had read about that. Cut off the nose, then the arms and legs, then beat the victim to death with the limbs. As if that weren't enough, the victim had their head cut off, chopped into a chunky salsa, then laid out for all to see in the middle of town. I had no desire to know where this guy had been spread out, but I had more important things to care about. "So he screwed up, and the daughter was still chattel." Jimmy and Kuan Li looked at me strangely, so I explained. "She was still property."

Kuan Li shook her head. "Oh, she not even that after he suffer Five Penalties. She worth less than bicycle for fish."

"Why?"

"When her *ba* alive, he would work hard so his daughter not suffer bad," she said. "He die, so she not much use for keeping her daddy in line, and she put in genpop." Now it was my turn to look confused. "General population, *lao wai.*"

Jimmy patted her on the bottom affectionately. "She watch lots of 'Lock-Up' on the TV, Tommy. She think she know everything."

"I do know everything about this!" Her voice started raising, a smile forming on her face.

"Okay, you two, as much as I'd love to hang out and watch you two bicker like an old married couple, I need to know what happened to the girl."

With the telepathic communication that two people who lived with and loved each other, they decided he should tell me. "She was sent across water," Jimmy said, "one of those washy washy places. Keep her high, keep her stupid. Got caught in raid three years ago."

Lightbulb. "Phoebus?"

Jimmy nodded. "Yeah. You should heard

Dragon Empress. Closest she ever got to getting caught. Dragon Empress got away thanks to friend of hers. He was a real dick. Had a thing for young ones, would go searching for them as punishment for those who piss him off." He shook his head. "You *gwai lao* not make good cops." As an afterthought, he said, "Girl die too. Fucking shame."

Oh godsdammit.

I left as soon as I could, and I made sure Jimmy called the folks watching the border so I wouldn't get my ass kicked again. Gods know I was already mentally kicking my own ass. Of course the general was behind it. It tied together, and made exactly as much sense as it should have, except for one detail.

Why did he want me to find his granddaughter when he already knew she was dead?

My mind raged a bit at being played. Flash money at me and I went along with the whole thing, stupid as stupid could be. I didn't appreciate being fed a bullshit story, especially when it came to family. This guy wasn't the cool customer I thought he was, and what was worse, he had no care about who he hurt in the long run, as long as he got his revenge. I understood to a point about the five targets claimed in this quest for blood, but if I couldn't stop this insane scheme and kept Chu-Jung from completing his task, the fire god might decide to give the area the Hicks treatment: Nuke the site from orbit.

After all, it was the only way to be sure, and there were at minimum two portable nuclear reactors and one nuclear power plant in Surry county that would render the middle of the Atlantic seaboard uninhabitable for the next twenty thousand years. For those playing along at home, that would kill about fifty million people in the first few minutes, and they'd be the lucky ones. Sure, I could be overreacting and Chu-Jung might decide to just cause a huge firestorm in the one of the most heavily-populated areas of Virginia and roast only a million or two people. He could feel generous, right?

Something was nagging at my mind, but it didn't matter; the general was playing with forces beyond his control. He had to know he was out of his league by a long chalk, but he did it anyway. This was revenge, and the fool was using a bazooka when a stiletto would do.

Stiletto, right. As I drove out of the Hidden City, I made a call. It picked up on the second ring. "The general there?" I said by way of greeting.

"You now understand." It was Chip.

"Your boss. Now." My voice was like stone.

"He is indisposed at this time, Statford," Chip said, his voice bored. "I will tell him what you have to say."

"Put him on and I won't tell him about your little fuck-up at the museum." There was silence on the line. "That's what I thought, pencil-dick. Get him on the godsdamned phone."

There was a moment, then a hissed curse. "Hold for the general." One minute and nearly a mile later, the phone clicked on again. "So you have completed your task."

"Yeah, I did, you senile fuck. Why?"

"You had to understand why I did it. Why it was necessary."

"So that's all? You wanted justification?" I nearly screamed into the phone as I dodged a car. "Gods, you old bastard, there were better ways of doing this!"

"Of the avenues presented me, this was most direct, Mr. Statford," the old man said matter-of-factly. "Chu-Jung will find the last one to blame and end this quickly."

I had one card left. "He won't, you sick bastard. The last one is with me, and had nothing to do with this. *Blameless*," I emphasized. "I know what those coins do, and I know what the gods do when they don't get their way. You're going to kill millions!"

"My granddaughter is dead, my son is dead, my son's wife is dead, my line is dead, Mr. Statford," came the voice through my phone. It was the sound of a man who didn't give a sweet shit about anything. It chilled me to the core. "Do you think I truly care if the rest of the world burns? If I cannot have my family back, why should I care? It matters not; Chu-Jung grows weary of the search and wishes to end his quest. He will end it today, and the fires will burn all, the guilty and the righteous alike."

"General, this isn't the way it should go," I said.

"You are saying I should have let them live?" He sounded surprised and hurt. "I believed you had more sense than that."

"What about the one who is innocent?"

"In this world, there are no innocent. I am

sorry, Mr. Statford. The gift of the Qin coins is the will of the gods. You of all people should understand that."

I snarled, "No! It is a mortal full of himself forcing his will upon the gods, and they will not forget such impudence!"

The shrug was almost audible. "Then I die after avenging my granddaughter's death. It is a small price." He paused as I said nothing, my thoughts racing. The old bastard was willing to kill millions to avenge his blood, and I had just played my only card: an appeal to his humanity. Of course, it turns out he had none left. "Perhaps we can come to an arrangement?"

Hope leapt up in my chest. "What kind of deal?"

"Bring the final one to this address." He rattled off a place I vaguely recognized, an abandoned office building in Newport News, complete with old parking garage and a falling-apart-at-the-seams structure that would make a great place to end things, one way or another. "The last will face blame and no one else will die."

"So you want a sacrifice?"

"Did not one of your people once say the needs of the group are more important than the needs of the one?" Oh gods, when the Big Bad brings up Vulcan logic, it can't get much worse. "I merely offer a solution more to your liking. It is your choice to accept it or not."

"Not much of a choice."

"It is your only choice."

I thought it over for a couple of seconds,

knowing that was really all the time I had. The pain in my stomach was from the barrel he had me over, and I hated every bit of it. What hurt worse was he was right. Not only was he right, he wasn't even being smug about it like most Big Bads would be. I couldn't even say I wouldn't do the same in his place. He was just doing what he thought was right, what was just, and if a few million people burned, then so be it. What did it say about him that he didn't even care about his own death as long as he got what he wanted. Then it hit me. Why should he care? He had nothing left. No family, no legacy. Just his hate and his revenge.

Like the Kingpin once said, a man with nothing to lose is truly a man without fear.

Still, he was giving me an out, and I needed to take it, if only to buy myself some time. "I give you who you're looking for and that's it? You call it off?"

"I will. There will be no further need for the cleansing fire."

"And the coins?"

"I will have no further use for them. You may do with them as you will."

I gritted my teeth, and I knew I was making a huge mistake. "Done."

"You have one hour."

"We'll be there." I cut off the call and tossed the phone onto the passenger seat. I hated being railroaded, but I rather hated the idea of being responsible for scorching millions of people even more.

Besides, I had a plan.

Chapter Ten

I picked my phone back up from the passenger seat and dialed Susana. She picked up on the second ring. From the sound of her voice, she apparently was not enjoying "girl time" with Dee.

"You owe me big for this," were the first words out of her mouth.

"I know, baby, I know, and when this is all over, we're taking a trip, I promise." Though the odds were against my surviving, I figured I might as well have a little bit of incentive to make it through the hare-brained scheme I was about to try. "In the meantime, I need you to get Dee to the Purloba Building in the next hour."

"The Purloba Building? Why?"

"She's the key to this, and if I play my cards right, I can stop some very bad stuff from happening."

"Like my taking the law into my hands?" Oh man, it must not have been a good time for her.

"Worse than that. The guy behind this is willing to do some very next level shit for revenge." I sighed as I passed the exit for my office and kept going. I needed all the prep time I could get. "I need you to get her there within the hour, or things go from bad to 'fire from the sky'."

"I'll back you up," she said. Gods, I didn't deserve that woman.

"No, you need to be as far away from that building as possible once you've got Dee there." My voice was firm. "This isn't negotiable, Susie. This is so far out of the normal it's not even funny."

She was just as stubborn. "All the more reason I should be there. You don't have to do this by yourself." Her voice softened. "This doesn't always have to be just your fight, Tommy."

I sighed. She made a compelling argument, and I knew she was right. One of these days, I would hare off trying to do the Lone Wolf McQuaid thing and end up with my ass in a sling with no one to pull me out of the fire. Here I had one of the best cops I knew---

No, that wasn't right. Here I had one of the best people I would ever know in life, not only wanting to stand by my side in a battle against god and mortal, but to be in my life and my heart. Someone who would not ever stop trying to help me, wanting to help me, even unto her dying breath, and even then she wouldn't stop. It wasn't right to exclude her if she wanted to be there.

"Okay, Susie, you want in, load up, hard and heavy. We're dealing with a guy who commands a freaking army of thugs. Follow my lead." I lowered my voice. "After this, we'll see if you want to make that a more permanent thing."

"We'll see, gringo." I heard the laugh in her voice. She was scared, she was excited, but too much the latter and not nearly enough of the former. "Little Miss and me will be there." The phone cut off and I shrugged. She was likely in cop mode and already looking for what she could grab weapon-wise that might help against either a god, a group of thugs led by a Chinese general who helped train a bunch of North Korean spy hunters, or both. I smiled at the thought; Susana was the kind of woman who would smile at danger and laugh in the face of death. That attitude was one of the many reasons I loved her, and why I always knew I could count on her, and why I would always come back to her.

I made another phone call as I took the exit I wanted. There was no answer so I left a message. There was time to prepare, which was good, but things were starting to move too fast, and I was flying by the seat of my pants. There were too many variables, and the fact that I possibly had to hand over who the bad guy wanted didn't sit well with me. I had to hope I could pull off a miracle.

Or, if I couldn't pull off a miracle, I could at least not get everybody in a few hundred miles killed. That would be a good thing. I could settle for that.

The Purloba Building was a victim of its own success. It was designed as the centerpiece of one of those town center types of outdoor malls, where land developers came up with the brilliant idea of having living areas and shopping areas all rolled into one place, then forget they have to have those living spaces reasonably priced. It was a common problem, and no one seemed to learn the valuable lesson that just because you build it doesn't mean they will come. In fact, unless it's something people can't live without, they aren't going to pay a premium for it, especially when housing could be found for half the price only two or three miles away in Newport News or Hampton. Hell, even Yorktown was cheaper with better houses, and even better shopping.

As such, the Purloba Building, located in that no-man's-land between Williamsburg and Newport News, was eight stories of empty office and living space, and had been for a couple of years. It was surrounded on all sides by storefronts that had been boarded up, restaurants that shut down not only from lack of customers but from a series of health department raids, and small parks that were overrun with weeds and the homeless. It was dirty, it was nasty, it was a few acres of desolation surrounded by the otherwise affluent areas which seemed to turn a profit.

It was a fitting backdrop to what I knew would be the final act in this revenge play. There wasn't much else to do but confront the villain, either kick his ass or otherwise keep him from unleashing a holy firestorm on a major metropolitan area in hopes of killing one innocent girl, and stop the likely destruction of the eastern seaboard of the United States.

Oh, and survive the whole thing. That would be nice.

I had arrived about twenty minutes before the deadline, and wanted to take a look around. The parking lot was cracked open everywhere, with grass and weeds bursting through the pavement. Broken glass glittered in the late afternoon light, with other debris as far as the eye could see. It was desolation, like I would imagine the world would look if all the people disappeared. There were pieces of paper and cardboard and plastic all over, adding to the scene of disrepair. The wind blew cold over the lot, uninterrupted by cars and people, whipping through my coat as I surveyed the area. It was a bitter breeze, and I felt it on my still fresh head wound, stinging and making me wince. Gravel crunched beneath my shoes as I walked around to the passenger side of the Beauty to get my shotgun to go under my coat.

I checked the load and stashed it beneath my long coat, the wind billowing out the cloth and chilling me to the bone. The coat wasn't to keep my silly self warm, but to hide weapons and give me a bit of an intimidation factor. While it usually failed on the latter, it did wonders for the former. I tutted at myself for the holes I had yet to fix from earlier that day. If I got through this in one piece, I would make sure and get my coat fixed, though that was the least of the things I had to worry about.

Sounds echoed off the walls as I approached the outlying shops, the stone sending my footsteps back at me. The boarded windows seemed to be mocking me as I got closer, telling me this was where all great ideas, all grand plans end up going.

There is nothing for you, Keeper, the buildings seemed to say to me. *Not just here, but anywhere. All your hopes and dreams are ashes. Everything you have loved and ever will love will be dust in your throat, and it will be all your fault.*

I almost stopped in my tracks. Something was even more wrong here than I thought, and I was walking right into it. I felt an intelligence, poking and prodding at the edge of my mind. Whatever it was didn't like strangers around, especially ones with ties to beings of cosmic power. I needed some backup there and then, or I likely wouldn't make it.

"Larry, here and now," I whispered.

The spirit appeared, looking rather miffed but impeccably dressed as always. "It is about time you remembered me, Thomas!"

"Not now. Bad things here," I said, not wanting to get into that discussion.

"You bound me to her home, not to her!" Larry hissed. "I could not go anywhere, nor could I tell you she was on her way to you."

"I know, I had a dumbass attack, okay?" My steps were less sure as the buildings, the land, the very air started to push in on my mind and my heart. "Can we focus on the problem at hand, please?"

Larry rolled his eyes and shot the cuffs of his blazer. "It is an *uyaga*, or evil earth spirit, Thomas. Not too terrible, but terribly annoying in the wrong places, and terribly abundant in this part of the country."

"Show-off," I chuckled, and I started to feel better. "What is it?" My pace quickened.

"It is little more than an annoyance that feeds off the dead interred in its place. Nothing to worry about."

Knowing what I was dealing with made it easier to shrug off the effect, and I resumed walking to the Purloba Building. "Now I know why this place is still standing."

"As I said, it is a rather bothersome creature, but effective." Larry kept pace with me as we crossed into the shopping area. "Now, why are you here?"

"Turns out the general was the big bad after

all," I said. "Kind of disappointing, actually. I thought it would be someone else."

"A pity," Larry agreed. "His reason?"

"Granddaughter died because of Jiao and her family, he's using the coins for revenge, doesn't care if he nukes the whole godsdamned world."

"Ah," Larry said. "That is rather pedestrian."

"I know," I shrugged. "I was expecting something more, since he's some big badass former spy or something."

"You have a plan, I take it?"

"Appeal to his humanity," I said. "If that doesn't work, I show him what blame really looks like."

"Oh yes, because that is always successful when dealing with someone who does not care if thousands die."

I looked over at Larry and smiled as I explained my backup plan to my backup plan. "Hell, man, you think I don't have a Plan C?"

Larry smothered a laugh. "I would be aghast if you did not have a Plan Q."

The store windows had been broken long ago by kids out of meanness or by vagrants wanting some protection from the cold. Most had been covered by plywood, but the rest were gaping open. As we passed, I glanced in the storefronts and saw people looking back at me, their faces gaunt and dirty. They stared as I walked by, probably wondering what this clean-faced interloper was doing in their home. I gave a short nod and continued on my way, keeping my hands out and free and myself very non-threatening. From what little I could see into the dark, they had been kicked around by life enough that I didn't need to add to their problems.

I made the entrance of the Purloba Building with no incident, which in and of itself was a minor miracle. The gods must have decided being jumped three times in a day was enough punishment and I could actually get where I was going with no real problems for once. The building's footprint was about thirty thousand square feet, which wasn't as big as some places, but with eight stories it was large enough to lord over the shopping center. The building was gray stone, which clashed greatly with the beige stores, and seemed just imposing over everything around it, like a tower of shadow and darkening dreams.

From what I remembered of the building, the first three floors were mostly an indoor theater, which was where I figured the general wanted this little meeting. There were a few offices and alcoves for defunct businesses and companies that tried to make it and failed, but the theater was the centerpiece. Some foolish planner had put apartments above the theater, which made no sense to anyone, including the poor sods who had rented there for a month before leaving due to insufficient sound-proofing. Once that happened, things went downhill fast. The apartments hadn't rented, the people started leaving for that and other reasons, and all that was left was a ghost town with an empty theater.

"Larry, do a quick run through the place, let me know if the general and his men are here."

"A moment." The spirit disappeared through the door and returned after only two minutes. "He is, along with a dozen gunmen, mostly armed with pistols with a shotgun or two thrown in for seasoning. It does not look good, Thomas."

"It never does." I pushed the door open, the squeaking of the hinges echoing against the other buildings. I kept my hands empty as I entered the main lobby; I would rather there be no shooting, and I wanted to make sure that the first bullet fired would not be due to a misunderstanding. There are a ton of other reasons bullets would fly, anyway, so why add to the possibilities?

The theater was built along the modern lines, with the lobby expansive and reminiscent of the idealized days of yore. Thick carpet covered the floor, likely a rich burgundy before years of neglect and abuse made it a murky mix of burnt black and brownish-red muck. The ticket counters stood empty, the plexiglass scarred and starred from malice or boredom. Graffiti from a thousand artists covered everything, with declarations of love, of hate, of ability all over any and every surface. The high windows that hadn't been broken simply for being so elevated let in the last light of the day, with shadows playing over counter-tops where kids had bought popcorn and candy and sodas to watch some stupid film about whatever made them happy. The whole place was run down, tired, dying. It was like being in a corpse that no one had taken the time to bury.

I stood waiting in the lobby, checking the time every couple of minutes. I had to ignore a call from

Harley Blackwater, but I had more important things to worry about than the latest news from the morgue. He likely just wanted to let me know he was still on for the camping trip in the summer, which was always more fun for him than it was for me. Whatever he needed to tell me could wait.

"Larry, go out there and keep lookout for the cavalry. I should be fine once Susana and Dee get here." I reached beneath my coat and flipped off the strap over my pistol. Just because I didn't want trouble didn't mean I shouldn't be ready for trouble.

Larry nodded and vanished, which was a trick I would have given a hell of a lot to be able to learn. No sooner had he vanished than the door behind me opened, squealing hinges and all. I turned around and saw Dee, dressed in her thick coat, her hands in her pockets, her hood up.

And she was alone.

"Where's Susana?" I asked, my stomach dropping.

"She had a call from some guy, said it was her boss and she needed to be at work pronto," came the answer, tinged with disgust. "Not sure what was going on, but she looked pissed."

"And she didn't call me?" I wasn't quite convinced, but I had a little bit on my mind.

"Didn't you get a text?" Dee seemed not to care as she walked up to me. I guessed that Dee was just acting like this because Susana had made it clear who exactly she was with me, which was something I should have done myself, but time gets away from me. Besides, Parkinson was an asshole, and he would pull something like that. "Anyway, she isn't here and she didn't tell me why I was supposed to be here."

I checked my phone and there it was. *That pendejo called me in,* it said. *Be there soon as I can.* Susana not being there put rather a kink into my plans. I had hoped a cop being around would have helped keep fingers off of triggers. "Okay, we improvise and hope Plan B works."

"Plan B?"

I laughed, figuring if things got too rough, it would be over one way or another soon enough. "Roll with it. Come on." We headed up the flight of steps that had once been an escalator, trying not to depend too much on the handrail that looked like it would crumble to rust at any second. That general state of disrepair was most evident at the landing, where it looked like a bonfire had been set but kept from spreading by luck and flame-resistant carpeting. There were small animal bones here and there, picked clean, along with other trash which I really didn't want to think about but did anyway.

We made our way through to the main theater, which was one of those IMAX jobs, with a three story screen and stadium seating. I checked left and right in the growing dark as the natural light faded. Small handlights were hung up, apparently in preparation for night falling, and apparently by the host. I really hate it when the bad guy is more prepared than I am, and this general was starting to bug me. What made it worse were the guys who stepped out of the dark alcoves, each with a weapon of some kind out and trained on me. That was not good for my peace of mind, and it showed a level of planning I should have seen before. I hate getting caught unaware, and that seemed to be happening more and more.

The general had to have known I was going to get involved in this. If he had done any bit of research, and especially if he was using the Qin coins, my name would have been in Day-Glo orange as someone who would be right in the middle of the whole godsdamned thing, and I would have tried to stop him. From what Larry and a few others, including my late client, said, I was getting a reputation for getting into the middle of things I likely should have let pass me by, if only to make sure no one else got hurt. That reputation, for good or ill, should have preceded me. Did he just think I would let something like a godly assassin walk around blithely murdering people? Was I not even on his radar?

That he had this much protection made me revise that opinion, especially considering they were pointing their weapons at me. I was very much on his radar, and he knew exactly what I could do. I'm damned good in a gunfight, but a dozen guns on me? I'd be chunky salsa before I even got my hand on my pistol. We passed through the entrance to the main theater, Dee and I, escorted by half a dozen armed men, their weapons not deviating from the targets on our backs, and with each step, I felt like I was missing something very important, and not just when it came to the general sending me out like he did. I knew he had known she was dead when he sent me out there. The question I had was why? There had to be a reason why he wanted me to find out what had happened to his granddaughter.

Then it hit me. He didn't just want validation or justification for potentially releasing an angry murderous god upon the human race. The general wanted to make sure he had someone who could talk back to one of the Almightys running around and get them to stand down. I was his backup plan in case Chu-Jung decided he liked killing too much, and the general knew I would make sure there wouldn't be any retribution on him by Chu-Jung or anyone else of a godlike nature. While I couldn't go head to head with any gods, my station and untouchable status gave me the clout I would need to shut Chu-Jung up and shut him down.

That sneaky sonofabitch. If he wasn't such a murderous bastard, I'd almost respect him. The thing is, it still didn't answer the question of why he was using such dangerous items when a bit of research and maybe a couple of bullets would work. Maybe he just wanted to prove a point. Regardless, it was too late to find out.

The main theater was huge, as befitting a defunct IMAX theater, with a screen that reached up about sixty feet or so and stretched about two hundred feet from one side to the other. Some thinking soul had reactivated the power enough to get the interior lights on, though they were rather dim. The seats the filled the theater were either shredded, rotted through or missing, opening up the entire place a bit more and giving the illusion of even more space. It wasn't that it needed more space, of course; it seemed one could have half a circus in the place. My eyes took in the figures at the stage, with the screen a dingy backdrop. The general was seated while Chip and Parker flanked him, and Chip, damn him, looked smug while Parker looked apologetic. I wanted to wipe the smirk off Chip's face, but the guns at my back kind of took the wind out of those sails.

"So, the great detective has returned." Chip's voice was amplified by the theater's acoustics, so it boomed and rolled over us. He sounded too damned happy to have me like this. "It took you long enough."

My eyes glanced at his wrist, still in a sling, and I smiled. "So how's the girlfriend treating you, Chip?" He drew back, glaring at me. "Okay, General, let's get this over with."

"Indeed. It is years past time this act of vengeance should happen." The general sat in a wheelchair, the cane planted firmly between his legs. He looked terrible, to be honest, as if he finally accepted just how bad it could be, and how easily revenge, in the long run, can kill you just as badly as those you want to destroy. The general looked as if he had aged a century since I had seen him, and it didn't sit well with him. My sympathy was limited, as he wanted me to hand over an innocent woman to be murdered.

I stepped up to the general, ignoring Chip's murderous glare. "It doesn't have to be like this, General," I said, trying Plan A. "You are messing with forces beyond your comprehension, and you may think you have control over Chu-Jung, it's a tiger by the tail."

"Chu-Jung may have me after he has done what

I ask, for all I care, Mr. Statford." He said it with such a lack of intonation that my heart actually pained. He really didn't have anything or anyone. "However, he has made very clear he wants nothing to do with me. He says I've no heart left, and such an execution would be spurious and pointless." The old man chuckled dryly. "You hear that, Mr. Statford? A god who executes people refuses my plea for release. Is that not pathetic? He is right, though. I am undone, unmade and unwanted by all I was. All I have left is one more death and I may finally let go this life and join my ancestors."

I finally got tired of the old man's prattling and whining. "She's an archeologist, for gods' sake!" I shouted, trying to break through his shell of self-destruction. "The hell is wrong with you? She's never even heard of your granddaughter!" I pointed back at the still and standing Dee, whose eyes were bright in her face, the hood obscuring her features.

That perked the general up, bringing him back from his reverie. "She?" He muttered something to Parker, who shrugged. "Who is she?"

"Deng Shen-jing. She's the last one you wanted killed."

"I know no Deng Shen-Jing," the general looked over at Parker again, then to Chip. "Who is this you have brought before me? Is this she?"

I motioned Dee to step up. "Yeah, this is her. Seems you need to work a bit better on your aim, General. She had nothing to do with it, and I'll be damned if I let you kill an innocent woman without knowing exactly what you're doing!"

There was some quickly muttered Chinese as

Dee moved forward, Parker and the general talking quickly while Chip stood silent. His eyes were alternating between blind hatred at me, and a neutral look at Dee. The muttering became loud screeching when Dee lowered her hood. She had stepped to my right, a bit ahead of me, and I couldn't see her face. Her left hand was holding the hood, her skin smooth with red nail polish on the fingertips. The general pointed at her as if she were a demon incarnate, and Parker put his hands on the old man's shoulders to try and restrain him. The two men jabbered at each other, loud and fast and I tried to get a word in edgewise, shouting to try and be heard over them.

All the while, Chip just stood there, looking back and forth and not surprised one bit.

Finally, after at least a couple of minutes of quick Chinese curses to which I would have taken offense had I understood them, the general got somewhat calmed down. "You brought that treacherous bitch here, Statford!" the general screamed. "You bring her in front of me and try to tell me she had nothing to do with my granddaughter's death? You are not that stupid!"

"This is her sister, General," I said, trying to not shout back after getting my own emotions under control. I had to walk softly. "Her twin sister."

"A twin?" Parker looked non-plussed, then nodded. "General, there was talk that she did have a sister, though she was supposed to be in New York." He looked quizzically at me.

"Hey, man, she's an archeologist, and the last curator at the Norfolk museum quit," I said. "I didn't know she was there until I found her in the office. It makes sense, though."

The general sputtered, then said, "You expect me to believe that? Where is Jiao, then?"

"Dead," I said. "I saw the body, General. She got nailed by Chu-Jung quite well, just how you wanted."

"Jiao? She had something to do with my granddaughter?"

I looked closely at the old man, and realized a limitation on the coins: they didn't tell the user who they would go after; just a random six people who might be to blame for a certain event. It didn't matter which six. Just six people with varying degrees of blame, or, in the case of Dee, guilt by family association. It sucked, but that was the way the coins fell.

"Jiao ran the brothel where your granddaughter 'worked', sir. Deng didn't. She is just as innocent as your granddaughter was. Jiao was the one who was truly to blame for doing this to her and to you." The velvet glove was needed more now. "Your granddaughter was used as payment for a debt to Jiao, and she ended up having your son killed anyway. I'm sorry. Please let this girl go. She had nothing to do with it."

"She was *zhifu de zhaiwu*?" The general looked at me, then at Dee. "And you are not Jiao?" Dee shook her head, her hair in a solid sheaf of night in the dark of the theater. It settled down to frame her profile, and I thought I saw a tear at the corner of her eye and half a sad smile.

"He means payment for a debt," Parker

translated.

"She was," I confirmed. "You gave the information to find out who did it. I found out that and more. I know who didn't do it." Looking at Dee, I said, "She didn't do it. Let your granddaughter's spirit rest, General, since the real culprit is dead." I nodded, knowing nothing more need be said as the old man pulled Parker close to embrace him. The general shook as he cried, letting out his grief into the younger man's shoulder. I started to breathe easily. I might not need Plan Q after all.

Of course, that's when a gout of flame burst from the wall, like a solid cylinder of fire coring through brick and concrete. A large hole had been opened in the screen, flames licking the edges before turning into wisps of smoke. The smell of burnt nylon hit my nose, making me gag a bit. That was followed by a sense of power compressing itself into something our mortal minds could comprehend, and it *pushed* itself into the theater. It was pure power, pure anger, pure fire.

Chu-Jung had arrived.

Chapter 11

As the fire god stomped into the theater, he got the attention of everyone in the room. It might have had to do with him being bigger and taller than anyone else. The flames wreathing his form helped a wee bit, too. Taking into account the stylized gold and jade mask on his face, Chu-Jung himself counted for seven of the eight feet of solid mass that blocked out the dying light of the day from outside. The stone was melted, puddled around his bare feet, and seemed to bother him not at all. His soot-and-crimson armor was covered in gold ideograms, looking like metallic flames surrounding his broad muscled form.

I heard shouts from behind me as the lights went out and the emergency lights kicked on, bathing the whole place in an eerie glow and plunging most of the place into darkness. Two of the escorts to my right opened up on the fire god. That's generally not a good idea if you have this crazy desire to keep breathing air. It's also a really bad idea if said god has both really bad anger management issues and poor impulse control. As far as the ability to project a frigging column of fire as big around as a school bus; well, that's just the insulting icing on a cake of injury.

I didn't even think; I just grabbed Dee and threw her to the ground. The gobbets of flame that flew past our prone forms engulfed the two poor bastards, carbonizing them instantly. It was so hot and so sudden, the metal of the guns vaporized. I had felt the blasts of fire shoot over me, and figured

I'd at least have a nice pair of blister lines from the passage, and this was from twenty feet away. Dee didn't scream, but I could feel her hitching in breath to do so.

Everyone who was just hired help ran, and it was probably the smartest thing to do. I saw the place empty of hired guns faster than roaches departing a kitchen floor when the lights come on. Parker threw himself in front of the general, his coat opening up, sweat sticking his shirt to his chest. I thought for a moment the poor guy was going to jump on the fire god, but thankfully, he was content to be a living shield, for all he was worth.

Running on pure adrenaline and instinct, I pushed Dee away behind a few seats, getting her at least some cover. I doubted it would do any good, but I needed time. Even thirty seconds to think would be enough.

Unfortunately, I had about three seconds, and that just wasn't enough time.

"Chu-Jung!" I shouted, my breath coming hot, sweat wrung from my body. "Stop now!"

And that's when the god of fire and executions looked at me.

Looked through me.

The eyes were coals of infinite blackness, smoldering at the edges of the mask. Smoke seemed to come from the creases and crevices of the mask and armor, yet I could see the stylized face perfectly. The heat came off in waves, but I could still see just fine, even if my eyes were drying out. There was an anger in those eyes as they bore into me, an anger that was not one of cause, but of course. It was his nature to be angry, to hate, to burn.

And here I was, telling him to stop.

"You speak to me, Keeper?" It was the voice of a forest fire, a volcano, fused in raw chaos and destruction. "You know who I am."

"Yeah, I do," I said. While he couldn't touch me directly, he could definitely make my life tough by setting everything around me on fire. Technically, he'd be in the clear. Technically, I'd still be dead. "Your services are no longer required here, Chu-Jung. Respectfully, I ask that you vacate this plane of existence without any further loss of life."

The god looked at where Dee was, hidden behind the seats, and then at me, standing between him and his prey. I could almost see the smile beneath the metal as he turned his head with ponderous slowness to the man who held his strings, who had summoned him, who commanded him to unleash a hellish implacable vengeance on six mortals. Chu-Jung lifted his hand up, holding another small ball of flame in his hand. Though Parker was using his own body as a shield, the general stood and lightly stepped around his bodyguard. He patted Parker's arm and shook his head. The old man bowed to the god and said a few very lyrical things in his native tongue. Tears rolled down his face as he spoke, and he talked as if his very heart was breaking. He fell to his knees and still he spoke. The general pointed where Dee hid and shook his head emphatically. I couldn't understand the words, but I could understand the meaning.

He was ending it.

Chu-Jung cupped the fireball in his right hand, palm up, and rumbled three words to the general. They had a tone of incredulity, but also of satisfaction. "Are you sure?"

The old man nodded.

And with that, the ball of flame disappeared, and the fire god dropped his hand to his side. The silence of his movements were unnerving, but I was just happy he didn't have that flash-fryer in his hand anymore. Without another word, Chu-Jung turned and left the way he had come, just a lot quieter.

I let out a breath I hadn't known I was holding, my head swimming from both dehydration and lack of oxygen. I put my hands on my knees, bent over a bit to get my head clear and filled with air. The general caught my eye and smiled slightly. It was an old tired smile, but it was someone who no longer had the weight of hatred and revenge on their soul. General Wu Zhe Hou could finally rest easily.

I love happy endings.

Dee spoke up softly from her hiding place. "Is it safe?" I nodded, my own mouth forming a smile as I stood up straight. My spine stretched as I put my hands at the small of my back. The popping noise was comforting, and I felt better than I had in a bit. Something about doing a good deed always makes me feel better.

"You have done well, Thomas Statford," the general said. "Thank you for bringing my granddaughter's spirit to peace."

"And thank you for being so wonderful," Dee

said, coming around in front of me and giving me a big hug. My back popped again and I gave her a hug back. Hell, even if it wasn't my girl, you can't go wrong with solving a case where the person you're trying to protect gets out alive, and the Big Bad ends up not being as big and as bad. All's well that ends well.

When the pain exploded in my crotch, my world went white. I hadn't been hit there in a very long time, but that didn't really matter to me because the pain was there, it was sudden, it was vicious, and it was totally unexpected.

As I collapsed, I felt my gun being pulled from the shoulder rig, and I couldn't stop it. I just fell to my knees and watched Dee turn to face General Wu, transfer the pistol to her left hand, and shoot the kneeling old man three times in the chest. The body fell with a stately bearing, the eyes wide open but no longer seeing. It had happened so fast the smile was still on his tired old face, and Parker hadn't even registered that General Wu's blood was all over his pants. It was an expert killing, completely cold, calm and professional. She then turned back to me and smacked me across the face. "You asshole."

Oh godsdammit. I hate when I'm right.

I managed a croak, found my voice again, and looked up at the woman, saying, "Jiao?"

"Jiao?" Parker shouted, his boss's lung material all over his shoes, finally coming to grips with what had just happened, but a bit too late. "You *saobi*!" He put his hand underneath his coat to grab his own gun, and was rewarded for his trouble by a quick gunshot from Chip.

Chip, who had been so quiet, so unsurprised by anything that happened, and who fancied himself heir-apparent, and now would be heir to everything the general had, since Parker, who I guessed was the true heir, was now bleeding out. I can be so stupid.

"Harley was going to tell me it wasn't your body, wasn't he?" I said, my hands covering my genitals a bit too late. "I have to start checking my messages more often."

Jiao nodded, pulling Chip close to her in a quick embrace. "You should have looked closer at my sister. Didn't you notice a few differences? My tan is a bit deeper, and my hair looks much better." The archeologist I thought I had known was gone. The madam was in front of me, like she had never left. No one acts better than an accomplished whore, it seems.

"I had better things to look at while I was there. I was a little busy trying to piece together who would want you dead. Besides, I knew the cops would be there soon," I said. My mind clicked over to more immediate problems. "Susana!"

Jiao sighed explosively. "Your little lady was alive the last time I saw her. She has a hard head, though."

I closed my eyes and thanked whatever god may have been watching me. "She's alive."

"You have terrible taste in women. Demanding, pushy, a complete waste of time." Jiao smiled. "I want her to know that you died because she wasn't here to protect you."

"So you let your sister die so you could have more time, eh?" I didn't care about the answer; I just wanted a few more heartbeats of life. "Who touched the coin first: you or her?"

"I did, but what did it matter, in the end? I gave her the life she had; it was only fitting I take it away." Jiao gestured with the gun. My gun. "Hands above the head."

"So why shoot him?" I complied, trying to figure a way out. "He was harmless! He was done with the whole godsdamned thing! You could have walked away."

Chip spoke up. "That would be where I come in." His toothy grin made his face the most punchable face in the universe.

"Come on, Chip," I said, derision in my voice. "You couldn't have come up with this on your own."

"My name, you *wangbadan*, is Li Chen!" I got pistol-whipped across the mouth. Yes, it hurt.

"Dumbass, I don't speak Chinese!" I shouted back, feeling my teeth and making sure none got knocked out. They hadn't, but blood flowed a bit. "I'm not wrong, am I?"

"I had the idea, yes," Jiao said. "I just couldn't get close to the old buzzard after what happened in the old country."

"But why? There were a dozen different ways this could have ended badly for you." This answer I did want.

"Do you know how paranoid my culture is, *hutu dan*? I'm sorry; you foolish man?" Jiao put her arm around Li's waist, careful of his broken wrist.

"No one on earth could get close to the leaders of the organization, and moving up in the business isn't easy for a woman from the back farms of China."

"She knew the best way to get the old bastard's attention," Li said, smiling. "We've been setting this up for years."

"Three years," I muttered. "So General Wu gets the notice that he's lost his granddaughter working for one of your establishments, you get the coins from Janey Rottencrotch here, he throws the coins and gets Chu-Jung to make it all happen."

Li smiled, making me feel even more punchy. He squatted next to me and tapped the barrel of his pistol on the top of my head. "You almost are intelligent."

"You just needed to make sure I got her to the endgame." Another thing dawned on me. "Those really were General Wu's men at the museum. They were trying to kill you," I looked at Jiao, "not me. What do you get out of it?" I said.

Jiao answered. "I become the head of my organization, Li becomes leader of the old man's. We pool our resources, and get more than we could by ourselves."

"China gets more than just a foothold in this hellhole you call home, Statford," Li continued. "We can take over this place more quickly than before, and there is little anyone would be able to do about it."

I shook my head, my hands still behind it, blood falling from my split lip. "So you bring in a fire god to kill everyone, then hope someone stops him from nuking you? Godsdamn, woman, you got some balls. Not much on brains, though."

She smiled haughtily. "I knew you would stop him, Statford. Your reputation precedes you." Jiao checked the chamber, making sure a round was ready to go. "I've dealt with long odds before, anyway."

"Yeah, I imagine you have. You knew the general in the old country?"

"I was a product of the Songbird Academies," she said, somewhat proudly. "He took me in, taught me all I would ever know about getting information from anyone I wanted, however I wanted. While the Academy taught me to use my body, he taught me to use my mind." She looked fondly over at the corpse of her mentor. "He left me in Korea to be his eyes and ears. I was more than that. I was the Yellow Death to all of China's, and by extension, North Korea's enemies."

I didn't let the name affect me. "Well, I guess you're proud of yourself. You killed your teacher, you killed Parker over there, you killed godsdamned near everybody, all for a fucking power grab with a limp dick over there who likes little girls." I sneered at Li.

That earned me another punch across the face. I was rather glad he had put the gun in the front of his pants. "You're sick, but I will be paying your little children a visit. They've earned it after all this, and you will go to your grave knowing you will not be there to stop me."

"A fucking power grab," I repeated. They both betrayed the same man, and for nothing but ephemeral power. "I'm really disappointed in you two."

"Look at it this way, Statford," Jiao smiled. "In just a moment, it won't be your concern."

"Oh dear, Jiao is alive!"

Larry's voice cut through the theater, making me jump. "No shit, Larry," I muttered.

"Is that your ghostly friend, Statford?" She looked around, not seeing or hearing him. The curse apparently had been completely ended. "A pity he will need to find someone else to care for him."

The click in my head coincided with the click from her pulling back the hammer on my Beretta. "The Yellow Death is what they called you, huh?" I said.

She nodded, pride flashing on her face. "I was responsible for seventeen enemies killed, with nearly thirty-five forced to leave the country or face the same fate." Jiao indicated the dead general. "He taught me well, but was always too cautious."

It was then that my phone played the opening bars of *La Marseillaise*.

"Whoever that is has impeccable timing." Li chuckled.

I pursed my lips. "Last request?" Jiao gave me a rueful look. "Come on. You've got me. I can't go for my gun, I can't stop you from killing me. It's just a text. I want the chance to say goodbye." Smiling grimly, I said, "Come on. I saved your life." Remembering the fight at the museum, I amended, "Twice. I'm just asking for a text message."

"Oh fine," she said. "Make it quick."

I pulled my coat open and made a slow show of pulling out my phone. Checking the message, I shook my head and tapped out a two word response and sent it. I looked up at Jiao and Li, who had their guns pointing at me still. "Wanna read it?" I said, looking at the two of them with unfiltered disgust.

"I've never read the words of a dead man before," Li said, yanking the phone out of my hand. His brow furrowed in confusion as he handed the device to Jiao, who read what she thought were my last words. She looked at me.

"'Have fun.'?"

They had lowered their pistols, and started to raise them in my direction. Two pieces of flashing metal came out of the darkness around us, embedding themselves into the gun hands of my captors. The screams of pain were almost in unison as the pistols fell to the ground. Immediately after, I heard a pair of high-pitched whines from two sides. One needle appeared in Jiao's neck, another needle was in Li's left arm. They instantly went rigid and fell against each other, their muscles locked, forming a living A-frame.

I stood up and picked up my dropped phone, putting it in my pocket. "Damned glad you showed up, Luc."

"How could I refuse?" The voice came from the dark, I couldn't tell where. "You promised *La Mort Jaunde*, and here she is." A shadow pulled itself out of the darkness from my left. Luc Bertrand stood over the body of General Wu. "I have dishonored you in my thoughts, *mon general*," he said reverently. "You were not the enemy I sought. May you eternally know the peace that in this life was taken from you." Luc glanced at the fallen

Parker Chou. "Ah, this one is alive."

I walked over to Parker and started helping him up. He yelped as I got him vertical. "We're walking out of here, Luc."

"*Oui?*"

"Just the two of us." I held the assassin's gaze.

"*D'accord*, Thomas." Luc snapped his fingers and sixteen people materialized out of nowhere. I knew there were at least twice that number in the wings, handing anyone who was stupid enough to try and interfere. "*Merci*. You may want to leave, as this will not be very clean."

My heart was hard. Jiao had come to me, scared, wide-eyed and marked for death. She had lied to me from the beginning. She had sacrificed her flesh and blood just for power. Li had made sure the man who was his patron had met his end at the barrel of a gun. Just for power. He had threatened my family. Just for power. They would have killed millions if this had failed.

Just for power.

Careful not to touch the shoulder wound Parker had, I half-walked, half-carried the hurt Chinese man towards the entrance Chu-Jung had made. "I didn't hear a godsdamned thing, Luc." While we stumbled through the hole in the wall, I heard Luc begin to speak. It was odd to hear him speak in a professorial air, even with such a chilling subject.

"This curare variant is a wonderful thing, *non*? It paralyzes the muscles, leaving the nerves completely untouched, the vocal cords unfettered.

"It makes sure that you feel it all, and you can let us know how it feels. Let us begin."

The screams followed us to the car.

Epilogue

Needless to say, I got Parker to the hospital in time. He lived and owes me a hell of a lot. I told him we'd be even if he did what he could to bring the whole thing legit. Last he had told me, he was working on it. I took it under advisement. Beijing wasn't built in a day.

Susana was also, needless to say, pissed, but less so when I told her that Jiao had run afoul of Luc. That mollified her a lot more than I thought it would, but I was just happy that all she had after the whole thing was a headache.

We were sitting on her patio in the spring while I took a much-needed vacation and she took a few days from the force. Parkinson had given her some crap about it, but not too much. Between her and Mac, they were his best people, and all three knew it. All three also knew that of them, only one was completely unqualified for the job.

I'll give you a hint: the name rhymes with "Barkinson".

So it was a beautiful spring day, and I had some money sitting in the bank that would cover my rent quite well for a couple of years with any other expenses I could think of making. I wasn't wealthy yet, but I could handle life for awhile. Susana sat with me that afternoon, holding my hand. It was a simple gesture, but one that filled me with electricity. We were relaxing after a long day of doing nothing, and we had a reservation at a nearby hibachi place, one we had gone to a couple of times when we first started dating. Even after all that, she wanted Japanese. It was different enough, I guess. I still wanted a burger.

"Hey, babe," I said, breaking the companionable silence.

"Hey, yourself, gringo." Her head was back, her eyes closed, her hand loose on mine.

"Been doing some thinking."

"Should I call the insurance company, or the book of world records?" The smile on her face took away all the venom.

"Been thinking about us." That got her to open an eye and look sidelong at me. "A lot about us."

She opened her eyes and looked full at me. "Go on."

"You know I'm into some weird stuff. Things that don't make sense in any stretch of existence. Things that aren't right, shouldn't be right, and should never be right."

"Your side of the weirdness," she nodded.

"Yeah." I cleared my throat. "What I'm trying to say is through it all, you've been there. You've always been there, and it took a crazy Chinese chick clocking you in the back of the head to keep you from me." I pulled my hand from Susana's and cleared my throat. "I've faced mad gods, demons, devils, angels and everything in between, and I've never been more scared than I am right now. I would face them all over again just for you." I stood, walked in front of her, and knelt. "Susana Magdalena Iglesias y Marquez," I intoned, reaching into my pocket for a small velvet box and popping it open in a single move that took me two weeks of practice to get right.

"Will you marry me?"

There were no words, nor was there need for them. She grabbed me, held me close and we kissed as I slipped the ring on her finger. It was the greatest moment of my life.

That night we met the family and friends at the hibachi place. Susana showed off her ring to my mom, my sister Jennifer, and my niece Hannah, while Mac, my brother-in-law Arthur Gage, Luc and Harley congratulated me, though my nephew Jacob intoned that getting married was a huge mistake, as I would get cooties. I assured him I had all my cootie shots and Susana was cootie-free anyway.

We all ate well, that night, and I announced that we would be married on a cruise to the Caribbean. I had already done the checking and the reservations for a spring trip, giving everyone a year to get things set up and timing planned. As I sat next to my bride-to-be, I looked over at Larry, who smiled at me proudly. I thought I saw a shadow go over his face, but I figured it was either a trick of the light, or maybe that he thought I was leaving him high and dry. I made a note to myself to tell him I'd always need him around, and all would be well.

My arm went around Susana's shoulders, pulling her close to me for a kiss. This got everyone clapping, though Hannah and Jacob made gagging noises at the gesture. Jacob even went so far as to poke me with a chopstick, claiming he needed to give me a booster shot against cooties.

Yeah. It was a good night.

Keep watch for the next chapter in The Statford Chronicles, <u>That You Do So Well</u>, coming soonish.

Once again, thank you for reading. If you want to connect to the author, check him out on your favorite social media!
Facebook: www.facebook.com/thestatfordchronicles
Twitter: @Walker875
Blog: http://walkersedgepublishing.net
Support your independent authors by leaving reviews and letting others know what you're reading. Thanks again, and I'll see you all soon. jgw

11285093R00116

Made in the USA
San Bernardino, CA
12 May 2014